# CAKE AND I SCREAM

## A Down South Café Mystery

Gayle Leeson

Grace Abraham Publishing
Bristol, Virginia

Gayle Leeson/Grace Abraham Publishing
13335 Holbrook Street, Suite 10
Bristol, Virginia 24202
www.gayleleeson.com

Publisher's Note: This is a work of fiction. Names, characters, places, and incidents are a product of the author's imagination. Locales and public names are sometimes used for atmospheric purposes. Any resemblance to actual people, living or dead, or to businesses, companies, events, institutions, or locales is completely coincidental.

Cover design by Wicked Smart Designs.

Book Layout ©2017 BookDesignTemplates.com

Ordering Information:
Quantity sales. Special discounts are available on quantity purchases by corporations, associations, and others. For details, contact the "Special Sales Department" at the address above.

Cake and I Scream/Gayle Leeson. -- 1st ed.
ISBN 979-8-9885385-3-0

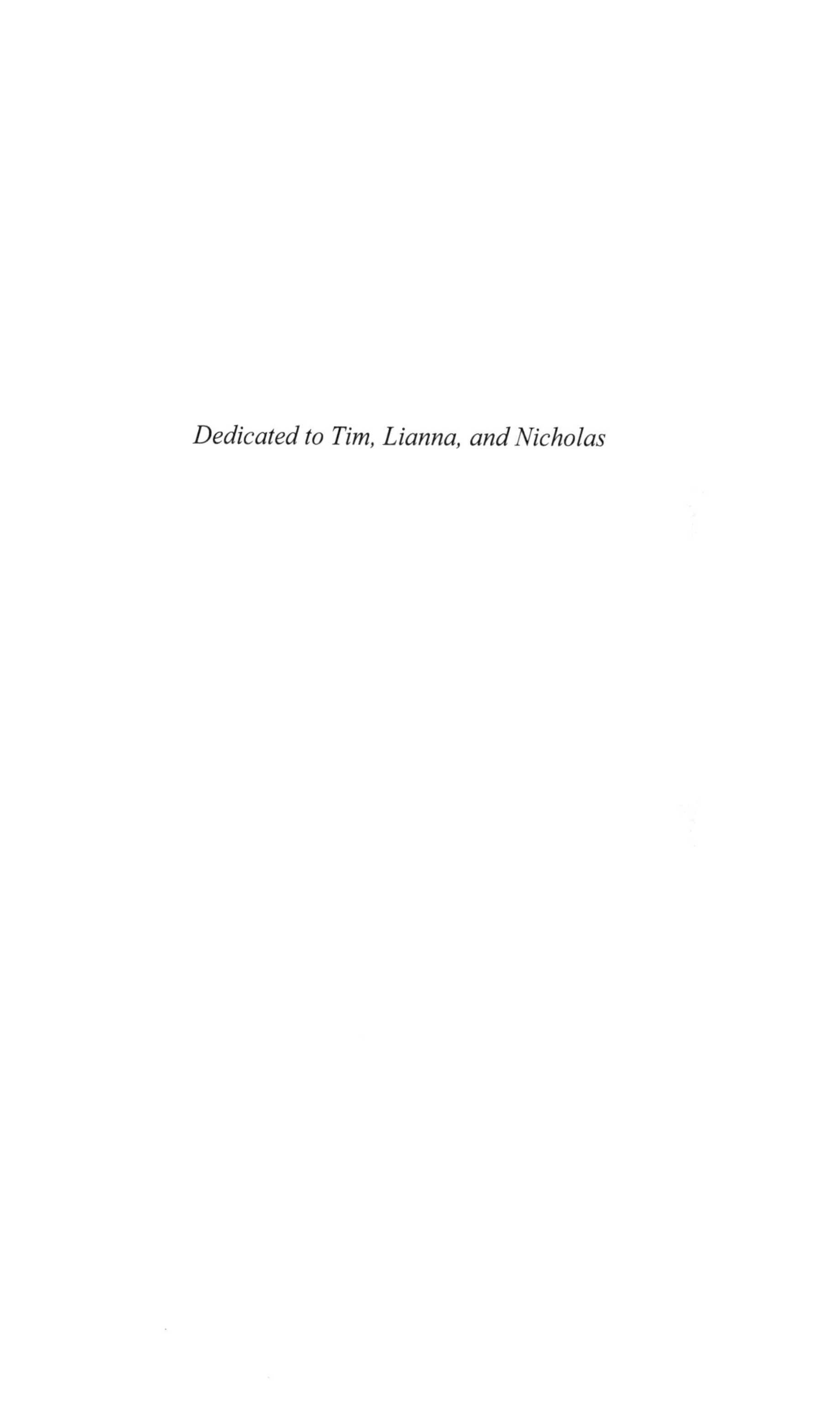

*Dedicated to Tim, Lianna, and Nicholas*

# Chapter One

"If we don't get there soon, I might have to eat this cake." Aunt Bess peered at Scott from the corners of her eyes to see his reaction.

"Please don't," he said. "Although I do see your point."

She sighed. "You're no fun. You were supposed to spaz. I think that's what the kids call having a hissy fit these days."

I wasn't sure what the kids called "it," but I was pretty sure neither *spaz* nor *hissy fit* was correct. However, I wasn't up to the task of arguing semantics with Aunt Bess. She, Scott, and I were on our way to Yona Ski Lodge near Beech Mountain, North Carolina. After their chef's wife had gone into labor, Katherine Donahue had called me in a panic and asked if we could cater the lodge's grand opening party. Even though it was only two days away—she'd called me yesterday—I'd said yes.

Scott had immediately gone into Super Baker mode, with an apron rather than a cape, and created a large, tiered cake for the occasion. Since *Yona* means *bear* in Cherokee, Scott had sculpted a black bear topper from modeling chocolate and had incorporated a trail marker tree and other elements that befit the region's lore.

I'd also done a bit of speedy research and prepared my menu to reflect the multi-cultural flavors of the early North Carolina region: tarte a l'orange for the French Huguenots, Cherokee fry bread, Scottish oatmeal rolls, German pork schnitzel, West-African-inspired Hopping John, Irish-roasted salmon, and English scones. What could be made ahead of the party was packed away in coolers and sat on the floor of the van we'd rented, along with Scott's cake. I was driving while Scott and Aunt Bess sat in the back carefully supporting the boxes containing the cake's tiers.

Mom and Jackie, my cousin and invaluable help at the café, had volunteered to run the café while we were gone. Donna, our part-time waitress, was filling in for Scott. I'd felt guilty about dumping the responsibility for the café on Mom until she'd insisted that I bring Aunt Bess along.

Aunt Bess had started dropping hints about wanting to go with us as soon as she'd heard about the ski lodge.

"Oooh, I've never been to a ski lodge. I've seen them in the movies, and they look very nice—people sitting around sipping hot cocoa in cute little fur hats." She watched me to gauge my reaction. "I have a cute little fur hat. Did you know that?"

"I did not," I said. "I know you don't like the cold."

"I would be sitting by the roaring fire. I might get too warm and have to go outside to get cool." Her eyes took on a dreamy wistfulness. "While I was outside, I might meet the ski instructor who'd think I was the cat's pajamas."

"Amy, may I see you in the kitchen please?" Mom's tone told me it was an order, rather than a request.

Aunt Bess was actually Mom's aunt. She was my great-aunt, but we both called her Aunt Bess. At eighty-something, Aunt Bess was what you might call a handful.

"You know good and well that I can't run the Down South Café in peace for two days—"

It was really one and a half, since Saturdays were short days, but I didn't interrupt her.

"—while worrying that Aunt Bess might burn the house down while I'm away."

She had a point. No one ever knew what Aunt Bess might do next, probably not even Aunt Bess. Besides, Mom could do with a break.

"All right." I sighed. "I'll see if I can talk her into going."

I returned to the living room where Aunt Bess sat watching *Jeopardy*. "Would you like to go with Scott and me this weekend?"

"I'd love it," she said. "I already know what I'm going to pack. Do you think there will be many Cherokee people there?"

"I have no idea. I believe some of Katherine's family are Cherokee. Why?"

She gave me a saucy little shrug. "No reason. I knew a Cherokee man, that's all. Back when we were in school. I could've married him."

"That could be your next Pinterest board," I teased. "*Men I Could've Married*."

"I'd have more pins on it than you or your mother either one," she said. "No offense, Jenna."

"None taken," Mom said.

"Why don't you want *me* to be offended?"

"You're still young." She flicked her wrist. "You could rack up several more pins yet."

Mom huffed. "Now, I'm offended."

Aunt Bess loved Pinterest and had several boards, including *People I've Outlived, Things I'd Like to Eat but Won't Make, Lord Have Mercy, Crime Scenes*, and *Things That'll Probably Kill Me*.

And now, here she was in her cute fur hat with her white curls sticking out all around it sitting in the back of the van giving Scott a hard time.

Since it was the middle of November and there had only been light snow flurries when we'd left Winter Garden, I was surprised when a police officer stopped us at the base of Beech Mountain.

"What's going on up there?" Aunt Bess asked.

"I don't know. A police officer has pulled us over."

"I'll get out and do the talking. After all, I am the charming one."

Glaring at her through the rearview mirror, I said, "Stay right where you are." I put down my window as the officer approached. "Good afternoon. Did I do something wrong?"

"Hello!" Aunt Bess poked her head into the front of the van and waved at the officer. "Did Ms. Donahue send you to escort us up the mountain because we're VIPs?"

On the one hand, I wished I could be swallowed up into the back of the driver's seat and hidden. On the other hand, maybe the officer would understand what I was dealing with and show me some mercy.

He gave Aunt Bess a grin. "I'm afraid not. In fact, I can't allow you to proceed up the mountain because this isn't an all-wheel drive vehicle, and you don't have snow chains on your tires."

"What? Are you serious?" I asked.

"Yes, ma'am. There's snow on the mountain, and it's illegal to drive up there without the proper equipment. It's too dangerous."

"We're ever so grateful to you for watching out for us," Aunt Bess said, "but we're catering a big to-do up at Yona Ski Lodge. It's new. If you'd like to come with us, I'll save you a seat by the fire, and we'll have hot cocoa."

Chuckling, he said, "I'd like nothing better, but you're going to have to get there some way other than this van." He took a card from his wallet. "Call this number. It's my cousin Sylvie's taxi service. She has a big SUV that will take you wherever you need to go."

I took the card. "Thank you."

"In the meantime, I'll need you to pull into that parking lot over there." He turned and pointed to a grocery store whose parking lot was already pretty crowded. "You can't leave the vehicle there for more than twenty-four hours, but Sylvie will help you with all that."

"Thank you," I repeated.

Waving goodbye to Aunt Bess, who gave a cheery wriggling of her fingers in return, the officer strode back to his SUV. I signaled, waited for traffic to clear, and drove over to the parking lot.

"It's a racket, if you ask me," Aunt Bess grumbled. "Waving at us like he's our best friend while making us call his cousin for a ride up the mountain. He's not got me fooled."

When I took my phone from my purse, I saw that I had a text from Ryan. My boyfriend was a deputy with the

Winter Garden Sheriff's Department, and he'd been warning me of this very thing.

*If there's snow on the mountain, you'll be turned back without all-wheel drive.*

There was no need to mention the message to Scott and Aunt Bess. Instead, I called Sylvie, who gave me directions to her taxi service on the other side of town.

Sylvie's Swift Rides was basically a covered one-level parking structure and a small industrial trailer. I pulled the van up in front of the trailer.

"You guys stay here please," I said. "I'll be right back."

I went inside the trailer where I found a young woman wearing jeans, a sweater, a puffy vest, and furry boots that were propped up on a coffee table in front of the ratty sofa on which she sat. "Sylvie?"

"That's me." She swung her feet off the table, stood, and held out a hand for me to shake. "Amy Flowers?"

"That's me." I smiled as I shook her hand.

"You say you're going up to Yona? I'm glad. I've been wanting to check out the new place." She ushered me outside, locked the door behind her, and gestured toward a black SUV. "Need me to help you grab your things?"

"I believe we can handle it," I said. "Thanks." If Scott's cake was touched with anything less than extreme caution, he'd have a conniption. And I wouldn't blame him. He'd put a lot of time into the cake over the past two days, and it was a masterpiece.

Sylvie went over to the SUV, unlocked it, and started it, and then she returned to see if she could be of any help. Spotting Scott, she said, "Helloooo, Gorgeous!"

"Hello," Aunt Bess said. "I'm Bess. It's nice to meet you."

"Nice to meet *you*. I'm Sylvie. And who are *you*, handsome?"

"Scott. Do you have third row seating?"

"Yes, indeedy. Do you need me to put it down?" she asked.

"Please." He looked at me. "If she could lay both rows of seats flat, then you and I could sit in the back with the food, and Aunt Bess could sit up front with Sylvie."

Sylvie held up her hands. "Oh, no can do, handsome. That would be illegal. Plus, if anything happened to you, I'd be liable."

"But your cousin is the police," Aunt Bess said, with a wave of her hand. "He'll give you a pass."

"I'm sorry. We'll take every precaution with your food and pack it in as tightly as possible if you're afraid of it spilling, but I can't risk having you sit in the cargo area."

"She's right." I placed a hand on Scott's shoulder. "If we'd have a wreck, your cake would be the least of our worries."

"Not mine," he said. "You know how hard I've worked on that thing."

"You're a cake artist?" Sylvie asked. "That's so cool. Come on. Help me put the third-row seat down, and we'll figure out how we can transport your cake without damaging it."

"Between you and me, she's either awfully flirty, or she has a little crush on Scott," Aunt Bess said as the pair walked over to the SUV.

Nothing gets past Aunt Bess.

Scott, Sylvie, and I carried all the food into the spacious kitchen of the ski lodge. We'd told Sylvie she didn't need to help—Scott had tried to *insist* even—but she'd told us it was all part of the service. I wasn't inclined to believe her, and I could tell Scott wasn't either, but I appreciated her help. Scott wasn't about to let either of us help him unload the cake, though.

Once we'd placed the food I'd brought into the walk-in refrigerator, Aunt Bess and I went for a tour of the lodge. Scott stayed behind to make sure his cake hadn't been damaged during transport.

"This is just like I pictured it would be," Aunt Bess said, taking in the lobby with the river rock fireplace that took up half the wall. "How cozy."

Floor-to-ceiling windows showcased the majestic snowy evergreens outside.

"Thank you." Katherine beamed. "We're awfully proud of the place."

"You should be." I ran my hand over the back of a buttery brown leather sofa. "Everything is beautiful."

As Katherine showed us to our rooms, we passed a painting of some Cherokee warriors who looked ghostlike. They were standing in a valley and were brandishing spears and tomahawks.

"Who are those spooky-looking fellows?" Aunt Bess asked.

"They're Nunnehi." She pronounced the word *nun-nayhee*. "They're strong creatures who are fiercely protective of the Cherokee."

"Huh." Aunt Bess lifted her phone and snapped a photo of the painting. "I'm gonna put 'em on my *Things That'll Probably Kill Me* board."

# Chapter Two

Checking my watch, I could see it was nearly five o'clock and that Mom should have finished up at the café quite a while ago. I called her to ask how everything went.

"We managed to save a few of the menus from the fire," she said.

"Ha ha."

I had the phone on speaker, and Aunt Bess could hear. "There had better not have been a fire without me being there to see those sweet firefighters."

The firefighters actually loved Aunt Bess. She often sent food to the station, and they followed her on Pinterest.

"Seriously, did you remember to give Dilly a biscuit for the raccoon?" I asked.

"As if Dilly would let me forget that. She was much more interested in what you and Scott were doing."

Dilly and her husband, Walter, were usually the first patrons to visit the Down South Café each morning. There was a raccoon who'd been coming down to Dilly's back porch in the evenings for ages to get a biscuit, and Dilly never forgot to take one home for him.

"What about me?" Aunt Bess asked. "Did you tell her I'm with them?"

"I did, and she was delighted that you were taking a mini vacation," Mom said.

"Oh, good. I am enjoying it so far…except maybe for those nunya-bizness things. I've put them on my *Things That'll Probably Kill Me* board."

Mom didn't even ask. "Rory misses you, Amy. He hears you talking, and his little tail is wagging like crazy."

"Aw, hi, Rory! I love you!" I paused. "I love you, too, Princess Eloise!"

Princess Eloise was Mom's cat, but she lived with me because Aunt Bess was allergic. The white Persian adored Mom, but she only tolerated me.

"By the time I get home on Sunday, neither Rory nor Princess Eloise will want to give you up," I said. "I'll have to move up to the big house with Aunt Bess, and you'll have to stay in my house."

Our homes are on the same piece of property. My grandfather had built them. He and my grandmother had lived in the sprawling white house with the wraparound porch on the hill, and Mom's grandmother had lived in the smaller two-bedroom ranch-style house. When Mom got married, she and Dad—and later I—lived in the smaller house.

When my grandmother had died, she'd left the house to Mom. Dad was long gone by then. Aunt Bess had already been living in the big house with Nana by then, so Mom inherited Aunt Bess and had to leave Princess Eloise behind. Of course, she still sees the cat all the time, but it isn't the same as living with her.

"I don't know about the pets, but that arrangement would suit me fine," Aunt Bess said. "Every day, I'd put in my order from the café so Amy could bring it home to me."

"You practically do that now," I told her.

"Sometimes I don't. Sometimes I have to eat whatever Jenna fixes…which is always good." Aunt Bess screwed up her face and shook her head. "But having the entire café at my disposal all the time would be nice."

"Speaking of dinner, I'm going to let you two go," Mom said. "Clark is picking me up in half an hour, and we're going out."

Clark was Mom's boyfriend and Winter Garden's only resident doctor. He was a real catch.

"Where are y'all going?" Aunt Bess asked.

"We haven't decided. Have a good evening, and I'll talk with you tomorrow."

After we'd said our goodbyes, I ended the call.

"Wonder what *we're* having for dinner?" Aunt Bess asked.

"I don't know. Remember, the ski lodge's chef isn't here. That's why I'm catering the grand opening tomorrow."

"Right. But we *have* to eat something." She flopped her head back with all the drama she could muster. "I'm starving."

There was a rap on the door.

"Maybe that's room service," Aunt Bess said.

We hadn't ordered room service. I doubted the ski lodge even *had* room service, especially not with a missing chef. I opened the door to find Scott standing in the hallway.

"I assembled the cake, and it looks terrific." He came on into the room. "There were a couple of dings that it suffered during transport, but they were easily fixable."

"I'm glad." Aunt Bess shook her head. "We went through a lot to get here. Who knew we'd have to change horses in the middle of the stream?

"It is odd that Katherine didn't mention the all-wheel drive law when she hired us to cater the event," I said. "I suppose she had so much on her mind that she simply forgot about it."

Scott stood with his hands in his pockets rocking back and forth on his heels.

"Why do you seem so concerned?" I asked.

He shrugged. "I put the cake in the walk-in fridge with plenty of space around it, but I'm still nervous that something will happen to it. Maybe I shouldn't have assembled it until tomorrow morning. But I needed to know if there were any major repairs that needed to be done; and had I waited, I'd have really been cutting it close. Plus, if I'd had to go back to Fred's or to Banner Elk for supplies, I'd have needed to know while the taxi was still handy."

"Speaking of the taxi, that Sylvie was making eyes at you something fierce," Aunt Bess said. "Did she stay while you reassembled the cake?"

"She did. Actually, she offered, and I accepted. I even offered to pay her more, but she wouldn't hear of it."

Aunt Bess rolled her eyes. "Of course, she wouldn't hear of it. She'd have stayed as long as you'd have let her."

"Not true. She got a call as I was making the repairs and had to leave." Scott gave a little nod of triumph. "If only the cake can stay in pristine condition until the open house."

"It'll be fine." I patted his shoulder.

"If you want me to, I'll go down there and put a sign on the refrigerator door warning that anybody who messes up that cake will end up on my *People I've Outlived* board," Aunt Bess said.

He grinned. "I truly appreciate the offer, but I don't think it's necessary. I doubt anybody would mess with the cake. I'm just really proud of this one—I think it's the best cake I've ever done."

"I'm proud of you too," I said. "You were a great decorator before, but since you've been working with Daphne, your skills are even more impressive."

"I agree with Amy, but I dare you to get the big head and run off to New York or somewhere to work in a five-star bakery." Aunt Bess flattened her lips. "You don't need that kind of stress."

"Now, Aunt Bess, Scott needs to follow his dreams no matter where they might lead him."

"I'm happy where I'm at," Scott said. "You're both stuck with me."

"Good." Aunt Bess smiled. "I'm happy where you're at too."

This was likely to be a long two days. I was glad to give Mom some much-needed down time. She'd given up her job to be Aunt Bess's full-time caregiver. Not that Aunt Bess required a lot of *care*. What she needed was supervision. She was like a child with eighty years' experience—she could get into mischief quicker than anyone I knew.

We went downstairs where Katherine was waiting. She introduced us to her husband, Bill.

"Thank you again for stepping up to help us out at the last minute," Bill told me. "We'd been afraid Calvin, our chef, might have to leave at a moment's notice, and we still failed to make a proper backup plan. You're a lifesaver, Amy."

"I'm glad I could do it."

"A few of the guests are already here," Katherine said. "Most won't be here until tomorrow. We're ordering pizzas for everyone to have for dinner this evening. We'll set them up in the kitchen, and we'll eat in the dining room."

"Well, if there's any leftover pizza, please don't put it in the cooler next to Scott's cake," Aunt Bess said. "It's very delicate."

"We certainly won't," Katherine said. "I did sneak a peek at it, and it's stunning."

"Yes, Scott, it's too beautiful to cut—almost." Bill chuckled.

"Thank you. I wanted it to represent the ski lodge as best as I could. I researched the area and learned about the trail trees, the yona, and Nunnehi. I even read a legend about Civil War gold buried in a cavern near here and incorporated that."

"That's impressive." Katherine clasped her hands together. "I appreciate your putting so much consideration into our cake."

"You're welcome," Scott said. "I derive a lot of joy from my work."

"I see the pizza delivery is here," Bill said. "Let's go dive in."

"Since your guests are arriving, would you like me to prepare breakfast tomorrow morning?" I asked.

"That would be wonderful," Katherine said. "Please prepare a menu and an additional invoice for me."

"Will do."

"Are there supposed to be any eligible bachelors coming to this open house?" Aunt Bess asked.

"Ah!" Bill wagged an index finger at her. "Are you trying to matchmake for Amy?"

"Heck, no. She already has a boyfriend. I'm the one who's single and ready to mingle." She fluffed her hair and walked ahead of us toward the kitchen.

Scott murmured, "Roll with it, Amy-girl. Just roll with it."

It was odd but rather nice to have an impromptu pizza party at a posh ski lodge. Scott, Aunt Bess, and I had walked into the dining room with our plates and had found everyone seated at one long table. Almost everybody had pizza. One woman had only a head of lettuce on her plate. I sat across the table from her.

"Hello, I'm Amy Flowers."

"Barbara Hayter of Hayter Realty."

"You don't eat pizza?" I asked, as Scott and Aunt Bess sat down on either side of me.

"Not anymore." Barbara plucked a leaf from the lettuce. "I'm recently divorced. My husband adored greasy, fatty foods. He and his whole—" She waved around the lettuce leaf. "—atmosphere was toxic, and I've left all that behind. Turned my entire life around." She popped the lettuce into her mouth.

I flinched as I heard the unmistakable click of Aunt Bess's phone to my right. Had she taken a photograph of the woman? I didn't look—*couldn't* look. I figured at this point it was best if I didn't know.

"You'll want to stay away from us then, Barb," Aunt Bess said. "We're catering tomorrow's shindig, and we have all sorts of fattening foods. Scott made the most beautiful cake I've ever laid eyes on."

Hungry as I was, I hated eating pizza in front of Barbara. But since Aunt Bess had made things worse by telling the woman to stay away from us, I went ahead and took a bite. It was wonderful. The crust was crisp, and the blend of cheeses was a gooey delight.

"Although I don't eat cake, I look forward to seeing it," Barbara said. "I appreciate art in any form."

"We do have some healthier dishes," I said, wiping my mouth on my napkin. "I guarantee that guests who are eating cleaner won't go away hungry."

"True, but we do have plenty of good stuff." Aunt Bess finished off her first slice of pizza.

"I believe everything we serve is *good stuff*, Aunt Bess." I glanced at Scott for some help.

"You bet it is," he said.

A sophisticated-looking man in his mid- to late-fifties said, "I'm eager to try all of it—the healthy and the decadent."

"What do you do for a living?" Aunt Bess asked.

"I'm a college professor of history and anthropology," he said. "My name is Charles Goodwin."

"You can call me Bess." She jerked her head in my direction. "These are my associates, Amy and Scott."

"Nice to meet all of you," Charles said.

"Likewise," I said, as Scott stifled a laugh.

To the right of Aunt Bess sat a woman, a man, and their teenaged daughter. They began talking to Charles about college.

"What majors would you recommend to young people getting ready to enter college?" the dad asked.

Charles considered the question for a moment. "Computer engineering is one of the best majors to pursue if the student is interested in technology. Of course, business and healthcare are excellent evergreen choices."

"You wouldn't recommend history?" the mom asked.

"Not unless the student is interested in a low-paying teaching career." Charles chuckled, and the rest of us laughed.

We all finished eating, and then Aunt Bess announced that she was ready to go up and rest. "We have a big day ahead of us tomorrow."

"We do," I said. "It was nice meeting everyone, and I'm looking forward to seeing you again."

When we got upstairs to our room, I asked Aunt Bess, "Am I mistaken, or did you take a photo of Barbara?"

"Of course, I did! I'm going to put it on my *Lord, Have Mercy* board. Who sits down and starts eating on an entire head of lettuce—without a drop of salad dressing or anything? That beat all I'd ever seen. A whole head of lettuce! I should call Jenna and tell her about it."

"She's probably still out with Clark. You can tell her and show her the photo on Sunday."

"I'll do that." She turned down her bed. "Have you talked to Jackie? What are we having for lunch on Sunday?"

Jackie and I always made Sunday lunch at the big house—it was our weekly tradition.

"I spoke with her before we left. Since I was afraid that we wouldn't get back in time for me to help prepare the lunch, she said she'd put a pot roast in the slow cooker."

"Oooh, that'll be good. Pot roast and cornbread. There *will* be cornbread, won't there?"

"There'll be cornbread and dessert," I said.

I prepared the menu and invoice for breakfast and emailed it to Katherine. Then we went to bed. Aunt Bess had wondered why I hadn't called Ryan, but I'd decided to talk with him in the morning while she was still sleeping. I planned to allow Scott to sleep in too. I could set the food up buffet-style and would be fine on my own.

Except for Barbara. I had no idea what to make for her. Maybe there was another head of lettuce in the cooler.

# Chapter Three

The next morning, I eased out of bed, showered, and put on jeans and a long-sleeved t-shirt. I'd brought a dressier outfit for the grand opening, but that wasn't until this afternoon. I wanted to be comfortable as I prepared breakfast.

I slipped downstairs and was glad there didn't appear to be anyone else up and about yet. I was looking forward to exploring that shiny new industrial kitchen. I mean, our kitchen at the Down South Café was nice, but it wasn't as extravagant as the one here at Yona.

The menu I'd prepared for Katherine had scrambled eggs, bacon, sausage, biscuits, gravy, and grits. I started with the biscuits. I easily found the flour, baking powder, sugar, salt, butter, milk, and a mixing bowl. As I was measuring out the flour, the man who'd been at dinner last night with his wife and teenaged daughter came into the kitchen.

"Good morning. Amy, right?"

"Right." I smiled. "I'm afraid I didn't catch your name last night."

"It's Doug." He leaned against the counter. "I'm a physical therapist by trade, but my heart has always been in the kitchen."

"Really?"

"Yep." He nodded. "I wanted to be a chef and even took a few classes in college. But Dad wanted me to be able to carry on the family practice when he retired. How could I refuse and break his heart?"

Avoiding the rhetorical question, I asked, "Are you happy being a physical therapist?"

"I am. It's tough to run a business on your own—all that expense and responsibility—well, I guess you know. But it's rewarding. Plus, I bake for my family, especially on the weekends." He made a jerky motion with his chin. "What do you say to me whipping up some of my buckwheat pancakes?"

"Um…if Katherine and Bill are okay with it, and if you have the ingredients you need, then it's fine with me."

He pointed finger guns at me. "I'm on it. I checked with Bill last night, and he gave me the go-ahead, and I'm sure that Calvin has what I need."

"You know Calvin?"

"Yeah. We go way back. Our wives are friends."

"I'm hoping to meet him before we leave on Sunday." I finished mixing together my biscuit dough, washed my hands, and put the dough onto a floured piece of waxed paper. Sprinkling flour on top of the dough, I began to knead it. "I think Katherine said he was attending the birth of his first child?"

"Yeah, yeah…a boy."

I couldn't see what he was doing since he was moving around behind me, but he was certainly making a lot of noise.

"Bill and Katherine were lucky you were available on such short notice," he continued. "Of course, I'd say you charged them a pretty penny—and I don't blame you. I'd have offered to step in with the assist had I known in time."

"I'm happy I was able to help them out," I said.

"I bet you were."

That comment had an edge to it, and I declined to respond. I was afraid that if I said anything at the moment, it would be to tell Doug to mind his own business, and I didn't want to make an enemy—at least, not at this point.

I was relieved when Scott ambled into the kitchen.

"Hey, Amy, why didn't you get me up?"

"You needed your rest. But now that you're here, would you mind making the eggs?"

"I'd be happy to." He raised an eyebrow as he looked between me and Doug.

"Scott, this is Doug," I said. "He volunteered to make some pancakes."

"Yep. Nice to meet you, Scott. These babies are so healthy, Barbara might even be persuaded to take one. They're delicious too. I'll consider giving you guys my recipe if you're nice."

"Gee, thanks." Scott turned his back to Doug and gave me a stare that plainly asked, *Is this guy for real*?

I simply shook my head. "Wait until you see the cake Scott has created for the party, Doug. He's managed to incorporate a yona as well as some other Cherokee elements, not to mention the legend of the lost Civil War gold."

"Lost Civil War gold?" Doug asked. "That rings a bell. Tell me more."

Scott explained that just after the end of the Civil War, a soldier used the Great Trading Path, which originated in Virginia and stretched across the Carolinas into Georgia, to bury some gold. "One of the last remaining trail marker trees in existence is on Beech Mountain, so I included that as well."

Other people came straggling into the kitchen as Scott was talking animatedly about the legend.

Bill, his arm draped casually around his wife's shoulders, confirmed that they'd heard about the legend around the time they'd started building the lodge.

"We thought it was very intriguing, if highly unlikely," Katherine added. "But to us, it simply added to the romance of the place."

"I believe everyone in real estate has murmured about that lost treasure," Barbara said.

"Where did you do your research, Scott?" Doug asked.

"Here and there. If you want to look into the legend, you can find a lot about it online," Scott said. "There have been many people searching for that gold over the years."

"I can imagine," Doug's daughter said, as she yawned into her palm. "How amazing would it be to discover buried treasure?"

"If I was ten years younger, I'd look for it myself." Aunt Bess poured herself a cup of coffee. "All the grading and digging that had to be done to lay the foundation for this place is bound to have opened up some potential hiding places."

"That's true." Scott winked at her. "If it hadn't snowed, the two of us could have gone on a treasure hunt."

"Oh, well, we'll have something to look forward to in the spring, won't we?" She spooned sugar and creamer into her coffee. "What will we do when we find all that gold, Scott?"

"We'll go to Tahiti, of course; that is, if you like the tropics, Aunt Bess."

"I do! I've never been to Tahiti, so it'll be a first for me."

"For me too," Scott said.

"I hate to burst your bubble, but wouldn't any found treasure have to be turned over to the state?" I asked.

"Nope. You'd have to split it with us, though." Bill laughed.

"Sixty-forty, our favor," Aunt Bess said. "Unless you want to help Scott with the digging. Then we'll go fifty-fifty."

"I'm not certain about the laws pertaining to finding buried treasure in the state of North Carolina," Barbara said. "We'd need to look into it."

"Where I come from, it's finders-keepers." Aunt Bess took a breath and opened her mouth to say something more, but she saw me trying to subtly but vehemently shake my head. For once, she conceded to me and didn't say whatever it was she was about to blurt out—more than likely, it was something about her and Scott not planning to give Barbara any of the treasure anyway.

"With my luck, I'd go looking for the treasure only to find it in a bear's den," Katherine said, getting a plate and silverware from the sideboard.

We spent the rest of breakfast joking about how we'd spend the money should we find it. Doug's wife said she'd put it toward their daughter's education. Their daughter wanted clothes and a car. Barbara said she'd use the money to go somewhere and make a fresh start—someplace she could completely reinvent herself.

"You could buy a farm and grow yourself some lettuce," Aunt Bess said.

I nearly choked on my coffee, but Barbara either missed or ignored Aunt Bess's sarcasm.

She sipped her herbal tea—the only thing she was having for breakfast—and said, "I could. And I could have a horse. I had a horse when I was growing up. Riding and caring for her was therapeutic."

"And horses like to eat—"

I had a coughing fit.

"—grass," Aunt Bess continued. "With a horse around, you wouldn't have to worry about mowing your lawn." She gave me a smirk.

"That's true," Barbara agreed. "It would be ever so peaceful."

While the lodge staff was cleaning the kitchen, I put on my coat, hat, and gloves and gave Ryan a call.

"Hello, beautiful."

I smiled. "Hi, handsome."

"Having fun?"

"For the most part."

Chuckling, he asked, "How much mischief is she getting into?"

"As much as she possibly can." I related the story about Barbara and her head of lettuce and Aunt Bess's remark this morning about Barbara buying a farm where she could grow lettuce.

"You have to admit, that's pretty funny. Also, I agree with Aunt Bess—who eats only a head of lettuce?"

"It *is* strange. *She's* strange. If I knew her better, I might be seriously concerned about her. It sounds like she's going through a lot in her life."

"You're wonderful, you know that?" he asked.

"Yeah, well… I'm ready to be back home."

"I'm ready to have you back home. I love you."

"I love you too." I was still smiling as I ended the call.

When I got to the kitchen, Scott was already there. We'd made as much of the food ahead of time as we possibly could, but most of it needed to be made on-site.

"Sorry." I was slightly breathless.

"Uh-huh." A slow grin spread across his face. "How is my second-favorite law enforcement officer?"

Scott's *favorite* law enforcement officer was his sister, Ivy, who was a crime scene tech.

"He's fine. As ready for us to be home as we are to be there. Or, at least, *I'm* ready to be home."

"Me too. This place is beautiful, but I'm looking forward to being back in Winter Garden."

After that brief exchange, we both got busy with our work. We worked well together. There was no one, except maybe Jackie, with whom I'd rather share my kitchen.

At last, we finished the food and arranged chafing dishes and platters around our centerpiece, which was Scott's cake. He'd photographed the cake in the kitchen before carrying it to the table set up in the dining room. Once everything was in place, I took photos of the entire spread to put on the Down South Café website.

"I'm awfully proud of us." I stood with my hands on my hips surveying our work.

"So am I." Scott gave me a one-armed hug.

Just as we were getting ready to go upstairs to change, Sylvie sashayed into the dining area.

"Oh, my goodness! This looks amazing!" She stepped closer to the table.

I stiffened and I could feel Scott's hand tighten on my shoulder. He was as frightened as I was that Sylvie would knock something over or grab a snack or *something* that would ruin the table before our hosts even had a chance to see it.

"Please! Um…come over here with Scott and me where you can get the full effect," I said.

"Okay." She moved to the other side of Scott and placed an arm around his waist. "Like this? Do we need to get huddled up to get the *full effect*?"

"Not really." Scott took his arm from around me and gingerly moved out of the so-called huddle. "Amy and I were simply celebrating a job well done."

"I don't blame you," she said. "Everything looks delicious and smells great. And your cake, Scott! Wow. Amy, he told me yesterday how much research he did before he even began baking."

"He's a perfectionist." I smiled. "Have you brought up more guests?"

"I have. Hopefully, my last group because I want to enjoy this party," she said.

"If you'll excuse me," Scott said, "I need to go up and get showered and changed."

"Me too. Sylvie, will you be all right on your own for a few minutes?" *Please don't touch anything*, I silently added.

"Oh, sure. I might go check with Katherine to see if she needs me to do anything to help her out. See you in a few."

She left the dining room, and I hurried up the stairs.

Scott was waiting for me on the landing. "Should we stagger getting ready for the party so one of us can stay with the table until Bill and Katherine come to kick off the festivities?"

"No, I feel confident everything will be fine." I patted his arm. "It wouldn't hurt to hurry, though."

Twenty minutes later, Aunt Bess and I were on our way to the dining room when we heard a woman scream. That scream was followed by another and another and another.

"Aunt Bess, go back to your room until I know what's going on."

"Not on your life." She went down the stairs so quickly, I was afraid she'd fall.

Scott was already in the dining room. Aunt Bess nearly knocked into him in her eagerness to see what was happening.

"What is it?" Aunt Bess asked.

"It's Barbara," he said. "Katherine found her dead in the walk-in."

"Reckon she was looking for some lettuce and got shut in or something?" Aunt Bess asked.

"I don't think so," Scott said. "I heard Bill call the police, and he said Barbara had been hit on the head."

"That's terrible," I said.

"Poor Barbara." Aunt Bess sighed. "She'll never get to turn over her new leaf now."

# Chapter Four

The police and paramedics arrived and gathered all the guests into the dining room. Scott, Aunt Bess, and I were sitting at a table close to the windows that framed the snowy lawn.

Raising his hand slightly, the college professor addressed the nearest police officer. "Good afternoon. I'm Professor Charles Goodwin. I overslept this morning and missed breakfast, and I feel my blood sugar is getting low. May we eat?" He gestured toward the dining room table filled with food. "I don't mean to be crass, but Barbara wasn't poisoned. She was clubbed over the head, correct?"

The supervising officer, a burly man of average height, looked as if he would rather be anywhere but here. "Who prepared the food?"

"My associate and I did." I stood. "My name is Amy Flowers, and I'm responsible for the catering of this event." I cleared my throat. "I mean, not this particular event, of course, but the…um…the grand opening party...which I suppose is no longer going forward."

"Right. I understood your reference without the clarification." He sighed. "I'll have our people take a sample of each of the dishes for testing just in case there's anything troubling found in Ms. Hayter's bloodwork. Then if you choose to assume the risk of partaking of the food, you may do so."

"Hey!" Aunt Bess got to her feet and hurried to stand in front of the officer. She poked his chest with her bony index finger. "The only risk you run when you eat food made by Amy or Scott is getting full before you've tasted everything. Don't you dare insinuate that there's anything wrong with that food."

"Given your advanced age—" he began.

"I'll give you my *foot*! First, you insult my family and then you call me old!"

"She called me family," Scott said, with a smile.

I sprinted to where Aunt Bess stood nose-to-chest with the officer. "I'm sorry." I put my arm around Aunt Bess. "I know you didn't mean any harm. We're all a bit *hangry*, I guess. Please feel free to make yourself a plate of food."

"Then you'll see how good it is and can give us the apology you owe us," Aunt Bess grumbled. "Gonna wind up on my *People I've Outlived Board* if you're not careful."

"What was that?" he asked.

"Come on, Aunt Bess. Let's get in line so we can eat as soon as the techs have their samples." I gave the officer a weak smile as I propelled the little firecracker over to the buffet table. I jerked my head at Scott, and he joined us.

"Wouldn't it be more polite to let everyone else go first?" he whispered.

"Ordinarily, it would. But there's been a murder, we prepared this food, and we want everyone to rest assured that there's nothing harmful in it. Take a bit of everything please."

"Gotcha." He patted Aunt Bess's shoulder. "Thank you for calling me family."

"You are family, sweet darlin'. And they'd better be careful with your cake. If they're not, I'll give 'em what for."

"Please, Aunt Bess, simmer down," I said. "I don't want you carted off to jail."

"You let them try. I'd have my fire department and police up here on these people so quick it'd make their heads spin."

Scott laughed, clearly enjoying the Aunt Bess, Octogenarian Superhero show. I was eager to change the channel to something simple and kind, like *Blue's Clues* or Sesame *Street.*

*Today is brought to you by the number 2 and the letter Y because there are TOO many people in this dining room, and I don't know WHY we can't leave and at least return to our rooms.*

"Amy."

I shook myself out of my reverie to see that Scott was speaking to me. "I'm sorry. What?"

"The crime scene tech said we can go ahead and help ourselves to the food now," he said.

"All right." I smiled and stepped forward. Was it my imagination or could I feel the eyes of the supervising officer on me as I filled my plate? Not that I blamed him. In his position, I would also be watching to see if the caterers skipped any of the dishes.

Passing the chafing dishes filled with Hopping John, pork schnitzel, and roasted salmon, I took a small portion of each. I then helped myself to the platters of fry bread and oatmeal rolls and selected a scone from the tiered tray on which they were arranged. I took a pre-sliced serving of the tarte a l'orange before moving on to Scott's cake, which served as the table's centerpiece. I was loathe to destroy it, so I took my sliver of cake from the back.

I didn't know how I was going to be able to eat so much given the fact that my nerves had my stomach in knots, but I'd have to eat a bit of each. I took my full plate to the table where Scott, Aunt Bess, and I had been sitting. After returning for silverware, a napkin, and a cup of coffee, I took my seat. As I began eating, I noticed that officers were stationed near each of the doors to enforce the mandate that we all stay in the dining room.

Scott and Aunt Bess soon joined me at the table. Everyone else got their plates and clustered into their own groups: Bill and Katherine; Doug and his family; the professor sat alone; and there were other guests grouped together that hadn't been here last night. I supposed they'd arrived this morning.

Sylvie walked over to our table with her plate. "May I sit with you?"

"Of course," I said.

She sat down next to Scott. "Isn't this the awfullest thing ever?"

"It's bad, but I've seen worse." Aunt Bess sipped her coffee, pausing to heighten the drama. Nobody could milk a story like Aunt Bess. "Why, only a few months ago, my dear friend, Mabel, got bopped on the head with a jar of pickles at the county fair. Who knew that just like that,

Mabel would end up on both my *Crime Scenes* and *People I've Outlived* boards?"

Before Sylvie could ask Aunt Bess to expound on the Mabel story, I asked, "Sylvie, did you see anything suspicious after Scott and I left the dining room? Or did you see Barbara come downstairs—whether she was with anyone?"

"I'm not sure," she said. "I don't believe I ever met Barbara, and there was a lot of activity going on. Nothing struck me as being suspicious, though." She shrugged. "I was busy looking for Katherine, so I didn't pay much attention to anything else."

"Did you find her?" Scott asked. "I mean, it was Katherine who found Barbara."

"No." Sylvie wound a strand of her hair around her finger. "I don't know how I missed seeing Katherine. I didn't know where she was until I heard screaming and ran into the kitchen."

"Did you—or did anyone, for that matter—hear *Barbara* scream?" Aunt Bess asked. "I heard Katherine shrieking when she found the body, but I never heard Barbara. She must've been hit from behind."

"That's a good observation." I frowned. "And that initial blow must've either killed her or knocked her out. Otherwise, she'd have cried out for help."

Aunt Bess lifted her phone and began snapping photos.

"Stop that," I whispered. "You'll get in trouble."

"For what? I'm taking a photograph of every person in this room." She clicked the camera button, causing Sylvie to blink rapidly in the wake of the flash. "One of these people is a killer."

"We don't know that. It could've been a robber." I looked to Scott for help.

"That's true." He nodded. "There's a door right off from the kitchen."

"And who's gonna come through it, knock Barbara on the head, and raid the fridge?" Aunt Bess lowered her phone at last and squinted at Scott. "A bear? Bigfoot? The infamous Ski Lodge Slayer?"

Sylvie gasped. "There's a Ski Lodge Slayer?"

"No. And as for who did hurt Barbara—" I couldn't bring myself to use the word kill with Sylvie staring at me like a frightened rabbit. "—that's for the police to figure out." I rolled my shoulders to release some of the tension in them. "I'm terribly sorry for this tragedy, but it's none of our business. This time, the calamity happened in someone else's backyard."

"I don't care whose yard it's in," Aunt Bess said, "it's going on my *Crime Scenes* board."

After the officers had spoken with us individually in the lodge office, they allowed us to return to our rooms.

Captain Spencer—yes, I'd finally learned the supervising officer's name—instructed us to remain in our rooms until the officers had questioned everyone.

Scott came to my room after he'd been interviewed. "Is Aunt Bess still down there?"

I nodded. "Heaven only knows what she's saying."

Grinning, he said, "I'd love to be a fly on the wall."

"Not me. I'm afraid that if I was a fly, Aunt Bess would smack me with her shoe and then put me on either her *Crime Scenes* board, her *People I've Outlived* board, or her *Lord, Have Mercy* board because—" I gave my best Aunt Bess impression. "—that fly looked exactly like my great-niece Amy in the face."

He laughed. "She'll be fine."

"It's not *her* I'm concerned about."

Soon, we heard Aunt Bess in the hallway.

"I do appreciate your taking the time to escort me up the stairs. I realize I don't look like it, but I'm in my eighties now…"

The officer must've given her the look of disbelief she'd been fishing for.

"It's true! I'm grateful for that strong arm of yours steadying me on those stairs."

I rolled my eyes, and Scott clamped both hands over his mouth to stifle a laugh. As if Aunt Bess had ever needed a strong arm to steady her on the stairs.

"How many of those weights do you have to lift to get such nice arms?" she asked. "Maybe I should lift some."

"No, ma'am," a deep voice answered. "You're perfect just the way you are."

Aunt Bess was giggling as she opened the door and waved goodbye to her handsome escort. She closed the door, sighed, and lowered herself onto the bed. "Too bad he's not about ten years older. Or, you know, that I was ten years younger."

I rubbed my forehead and asked how her conversation with Captain Spencer had gone.

"It went fine. I told him I got the impression right off the bat that Barbara was an oddball. I mean, who eats a head of lettuce for her entire meal—without even a drop of salad dressing? I asked him that very question, and he didn't seem to know the answer. Especially after I told him the rest of us were having pizza."

Opening my mouth to ask another question, I closed it again when Aunt Bess continued speaking.

"I suggested the poor woman might have been on drugs or something and told him he should be sure to have a full tox screen done."

"Ivy would be proud of you," Scott said.

"Tell her, would you?" She grinned. "I'd do it myself, but I don't want her to think I'm bragging or being self-congratulatory."

"What did Captain Spencer think of your idea about the tox screen?" I asked.

"He thought it was wise…said he'd be sure to request a battery of tests," she said. "However, he didn't think it would make much difference whether she was on drugs or not because the cause of her death was most likely the blow from that cast-iron skillet."

Neither Captain Spencer nor anyone else had mentioned to Scott or me that Barbara had been killed with a cast-iron skillet. We'd understood that the poor woman had been hit with a blunt object, but no one had said *skillet.*

"Are you sure it was a skillet that was used to kill her?" I asked Aunt Bess.

"Of course, I'm sure. *Skillet* isn't a commonly misheard word, and I'm not hard of hearing even if it was."

"I know you aren't." I took a seat beside her. "It's just that Captain Spencer told me Barbara was hit from behind with a blunt object."

"That's what he told me too," Scott said. "A blunt object—those were his exact words."

"Well, you can't get much blunter than a cast-iron skillet," Aunt Bess said.

"I feel like my concern—and Scott's—is not over what weapon was used but instead over the fact that Captain Spencer didn't disclose the weapon to us. It makes me believe he sees Scott and me as suspects, and that's why he didn't go into specifics."

Aunt Bess scoffed. "Poppycock! If he truly suspected the two of you, he'd have told you to see if you'd flinch when he mentioned it. Besides, he's bound to realize the three of us would get together and compare notes."

"That's true." Scott sat on the room's only chair and raked his fingers through his hair. "But Amy and I were the only ones who were working in the kitchen this morning…although I didn't use any cast-iron skillets. Did you?"

"We weren't the only ones working in there," I said. "Doug came in before breakfast and made buckwheat pancakes."

"That's right he did. Did he use a cast-iron?" Scott asked. "I can't remember."

"I believe he did." I looked up at the ceiling as I tried to remember. In my mind's eye, I could see Doug standing at the stove pouring pancake batter into a cast-iron skillet. "Yes, he did. He was familiar with Calvin's kitchen setup too. He seemed to know where everything was located."

"Even if he was using a cast-iron skillet, it's hard to imagine he disliked Barbara enough to kill her after knowing her for only a few hours." Aunt Bess flipped her palms. "I mean, I'm sure we all thought she was weird, but she seemed nice enough."

"I agree," Scott said. "You've got an excellent point, Aunt Bess. The person who killed Barbara is bound to have either known her prior to coming here or else she caught the person doing something they shouldn't have been."

Shaking her head and setting her curls to bouncing, Aunt Bess said, "I'm still not buying the prowler theory. It's too blasted hard to get up and down the mountain on these icy roads. If I wanted to rob someplace, I believe I could find a more convenient target."

"And one with more business," Scott added. "This is an incredible lodge, but it isn't even filled to capacity yet."

"Yeah, I agree that a prowler makes no sense whatsoever," I said. "I wonder where Barbara's ex-husband might be."

"Far away from here where he can be alibied is my guess," Aunt Bess said. "Likely hired one of these guests to do his dirty work."

"Well, as soon as we're cleared and given permission to leave, we can—thankfully—leave this mess for the Beech Mountain Police Department to clean up." I gave a firm nod. "And I'm sure they'll find the culprit and bring him or her to justice in no time."

"I'm not as happy about that as you are." Aunt Bess plucked her compact from the nightstand and opened it. "I informed Captain Spencer that I have experience in solving these types of crimes and that I'd be happy to consult should he need me." She powdered her nose. "And I feel fairly certain he needs me."

My eyes flew to Scott's. His were filled with amusement.

"Relax, Amy-girl." He winked. "I'm confident we'll be home tomorrow as planned."

I wished I was as sure of that as he seemed to be.

# Chapter Five

Sylvie arrived the next morning to take us back to the van we'd rented for the trip. We'd packed up our chafing dishes and other serving trays but had left the remainder of the food, of course. Katherine and Bill had paid well for it. I was sorry, though, that their grand opening party had been ruined. I'd attempted to have Katherine deduct twenty percent of our fee, but she wouldn't hear of it.

"You went above and beyond," she said. "I wouldn't dream of undercutting your pay due to an unexpected...circumstance."

"Thank you. If there's anything you need from me or if I can be of assistance in the future, please don't hesitate to call on me."

"Of course." She hugged me. "I appreciate your hard work and dedication, Amy."

I was sorry we hadn't been able to meet Calvin, but he'd not yet arrived when Sylvie came to take us to the van.

"It was so crazy about that lady," Sylvie said now as she maneuvered her SUV down the mountain.

Scott, Aunt Bess, and I had discussed it last night and had decided not to dole out any theories we had on Barbara's murder, especially not to Sylvie. It wasn't that I trusted her any less than the guests we'd met, but she'd made it abundantly clear that she enjoyed talking. There wasn't a doubt in my mind that Barbara's murder would be her favorite topic of conversation for the next few days, and I didn't want anything we might say to come back and bite us.

I answered Sylvie as noncommittally as I could. "It sure was."

Scott figuratively took the baton and took off down the track, beautifully changing the subject. "I believe my cake was a hit, you know, all things considered."

"How could it not be? It was wonderful." Sylvie turned slightly to give Scott a broad smile. "I'm sorry I didn't get a slice of it yesterday."

"Watch out." I drew her attention back to the road.

She squinted. "What did you see?"

"I…um…I'm not sure." I shrugged.

I hadn't seen anything, but I hadn't wanted her distraction to cause us to wreck.

I'd taken the passenger seat—to Sylvie's obvious dismay—putting Scott and Aunt Bess in the second row of seats. My hope was that without Scott sitting beside her, Sylvie would pay more attention to the road. It appeared my reasoning was faulty.

"Why didn't you get a piece of cake?" Scott asked.

"I was too full from all of the other food," she said. "Everything was delicious."

"Thank you," I said. "I hope you'll tell your friends about us."

I looked around to see what Aunt Bess was doing. It wasn't like her to be so quiet. She'd dozed off with her head resting against the window.

Following my gaze, Scott smiled softly as he put an arm around her and pulled her gently against his side. "I'm guessing that glass is cold."

Aunt Bess woke up enough to mumble, "Such a good boy."

"Lucky Bess," Sylvie muttered under her breath.

"Do you think Aunt Bess was more upset about Barbara's murder than she let on, Amy?" Scott asked quietly. "Did she not sleep well last night?"

"She didn't sleep well because she was updating her Pinterest boards and trying to find out as much as she could about Barbara and her ex-husband," I said. "She kept me awake while she was at it."

"What did she find out?" Sylvie asked.

"No idea." I tried—and failed—to stifle a yawn "She's convinced Captain Spencer is going to need her help, but I'm happy to be leaving the entire situation behind us."

"I am too," Scott said. "I'm ready to dive into some holiday baking with no distractions. In addition to the cakes, pies, and cupcakes I'll be making for the café, I'm starting to get a lot of outside orders."

"That's great," I said. "I'll be happy to lend a hand if you need me."

"I appreciate the offer, but I believe Leslie and I can handle it."

"Who's Leslie?" Sylvie asked.

I was kinda hoping he either wouldn't answer her until we were safely off the mountain or wouldn't elaborate on his relationship with Leslie, but he was too polite for either.

"She's an incredibly talented cake artist I've been seeing," he said. "Her aunt, Daphne, is famous for her cakes in Brea Ridge. Leslie and I met while we were both taking classes from Daphne."

"That's nice."

Sylvie's tone belied her words. The rest of the drive down the mountain was quiet except for Aunt Bess's occasional snoring.

Finally, we were in the van and on our way home. We'd paid Sylvie, thanked her for all her help, and encouraged her to stop in at the Down South Café if she ever found herself in Winter Garden, Virginia. She'd asked us to call her—she'd been looking at Scott at the time—if and when we ever returned to Beech Mountain.

As beautiful as the area and Yona Ski Lodge were, this experience hadn't been what we'd bargained for when we'd sat out on Friday morning. With the possible exception of Aunt Bess, who'd have loved to have stuck around and played detective, we were delighted to return to Winter Garden.

We stopped by the café where Scott had left his car parked, and then Aunt Bess and I headed to my house. As eager as I was to see Mom, I was looking forward to seeing Rory even more. After all, I wouldn't have to immediately explain to him that there'd been a murder at the ski lodge.

In a perfect world, I'd be able to greet Mom, Rory, and Princess Eloise—who'd likely pout at me for days, not for leaving but for coming back and relieving Mom of her duties—and I could ask Mom about Jackie, Roger, Donna, Luis, Homer, Dilly, Walter, and everything else I wanted to hear about the café without having to talk about

Barbara, cast-iron skillets, and suspects. But I knew Aunt Bess too well to believe that my perfect world scenario would come to pass.

In my driveway, I cut off the van's engine. "Aunt Bess, I can take you on up to the big house if you'd like. I know how allergic you are to Princess Eloise."

"I appreciate your thoughtfulness, but I figured we'd stop here first, so I took an allergy pill this morning."

By the time I got out of the van and gathered the boxes I needed to take inside, Aunt Bess had already gone into the house.

Walking inside, I placed the boxes onto the floor and scooped up Rory, who had raced to greet me. I laughed as he licked my chin.

"What's this about a murder?" Mom asked.

Princess Eloise sat on Mom's lap, scowling at me for whatever I'd done to upset Mom.

"I'm trying to tell you, Jenna, if you'll listen," Aunt Bess said. "Maybe we can talk about it over lunch. I'm as hungry as a bear—or a *yona*." She grinned at me, pleased to have learned a Cherokee word.

"That's a good idea." I kissed the top of Rory's head before putting his wiggly body onto the floor. "You two go ahead. I'll be right there."

Mom hugged me, enveloping me in her familiar amber and jasmine-scented perfume. "I'm glad you're home safe."

"Me, too. Thank you for holding down the fort."

She smiled at Princess Eloise who was sitting on the sofa, obviously expecting Mom to return. "I enjoyed it."

Mom and Aunt Bess took Mom's car up to the big house. I sat on the sofa beside Princess Eloise, but she flicked her tail in the air, hopped down, and stalked into the kitchen.

It felt good to have a moment to myself for the first time all weekend. I stretched out and gathered Rory next to me.

Taking out my phone, I texted Ryan: *I'm home. I love you and hope you're having a good day.*

His reply: *It's better now. Are you up for some company when I get off work?*

Me: *Yes! I can hardly wait to see you. I'll make dinner.*

Him: *We can go out if you'd prefer.*

Me: *No, thank you. I want to be home.*

Him: *Hopefully, there won't be any major crimes to make me run late.*

He'd added a winking face and a heart at the end of that message. I texted back a heart and decided not to tell him that I'd already had enough major crimes for one weekend. I'd fill him in on that fun fact in person.

# Chapter Six

I poured the tea and lemonade as Jackie put the plates on the table. Mom was gathering the silverware, and Aunt Bess was telling us who she suspected—or not—of killing Barbara.

"I don't think it was Bill or Katherine," she said, "although Katherine *did* find the body. You know, sometimes killers do that. They murder a person and then scream to high heaven as if they merely happened to stumble upon them. But I don't think Katherine would've done that."

"Why not?" Jackie asked.

"The grand opening of the ski lodge was too important to their business. If she or Bill had wanted to knock Barbara on the head, they'd have done it at another time and place."

I had to hand it to Aunt Bess. She was becoming quite the Miss Marple.

"Unless they wanted all those witnesses to alibi them," Mom said.

"Jenna, Jenna, Jenna..." Aunt Bess shook her head. "Because of the murder, everyone at the grand opening celebration, which didn't actually happen, is now talking about Barbara, her lettuce, and her death, rather than the beautiful new ski lodge. Why would Katherine and Bill want that?"

"Her *lettuce*?" Jackie asked.

"Oh, yes! I haven't told you the best part yet, have I? Lettuce was all she ate."

As Aunt Bess continued to rant about the lettuce to Jackie, I gently pulled Mom aside and whispered, "I need to make sure you have more time to yourself."

She laughed and gave me a hug.

When I tuned back into Aunt Bess, she was saying that she didn't really suspect Sylvie of the crime either.

"Sylvie is the gal who drove us up and down the mountain in her very large SUV. I pretended to sleep on the way down the mountain this morning, so I could observe her."

"You were not pretending!" I gaped at her. "I heard you snoring."

"Acting!" She raised her arm with a flourish.

I held up my hands in defense. “You had us all fooled. But why don’t you suspect Sylvie?”

“She only ferried us and a few of the other guests back and forth,” Aunt Bess said. “She wasn’t really supposed to be at the lodge.” She narrowed her eyes. “Why? Do *you* suspect her?”

Shrugging slightly, I said, “She, and anyone else at the lodge, could have a connection to Barbara that we don’t know about. You know the old saying about everyone being a suspect.”

“I’m lost with all this talk about Barbara, suspects, and lettuce,” Jackie said. “Could we please change the subject to what a terrific job Aunt Jenna and I did running the café?

“Gladly.” I ladled pot roast onto our plates. “Tell me everything.”

Thankfully, we always made enough food for Sunday lunch to have leftovers for half the town for dinner. Mom and Aunt Bess had plenty, even with Clark joining them; Jackie took home dinner for her and her boyfriend, Roger; and I had enough to feed Ryan and me. Ours was warming in a Dutch oven on the stovetop when Ryan arrived.

I threw myself into his arms, and he picked me off the ground and twirled me around. We were laughing when he sat me back onto the floor. At his feet, Rory waited with a tennis ball while Princess Eloise wound around Ryan's ankles.

"They missed you more than they did me," I said.

"I doubt that." He took the tennis ball and rolled it across the floor, and Rory happily scampered after it. "Dinner smells wonderful." He stroked Princess Eloise's head.

"It will be warm enough to eat in just a few minutes." I took his jacket and hung it up on the coat tree by the door. "Tell me about your weekend."

"Well, it was terribly boring. My beautiful girlfriend took off to a fancy ski lodge with her great aunt and her co-worker, leaving me here to fight crime and brood like some wannabe dark knight."

"Ha, ha, Batman." I took his hand and led him over to the sofa. "You only *think* I was at the ski lodge with Aunt Bess and Scott. It turned out, I was there with Miss Marple and…I don't know who to call Scott—a cross between Eeyore and Marcel Desaulniers, maybe? He was one stressed-out cake designer."

He laughed as we sat down. "That's intriguing. Tell me more."

"Let's just say the grand opening party didn't go as planned. In fact, it didn't *go* at all actually." I took a deep breath and told him about Barbara being found murdered in the cooler. "Poor Scott didn't want to say anything about it, but I could tell he was bummed about not being able to showcase his cake properly after putting so much research and work into it. It was exceptionally detailed."

"And Aunt Bess?"

"She told Captain Spencer that she'd be happy to consult with him should he need her services."

Throwing back his head, he guffawed. "That woman is one in a million."

"You're telling me. I was concerned for a while that the captain considered Scott and me to be suspects, and I was relieved when he allowed us to leave the lodge."

"Why would you feel you were suspected over everyone else at the lodge?" he asked. "You had no connection to Barbara."

"That's just it. No one seemed to have any prior association with her, and she was killed with a cast-iron skillet."

"Someone there is bound to have had a connection with the victim." He leaned forward, resting his forearms on his thighs. "Unless it was a robbery gone wrong. Was anything taken?"

Rory brought the tennis ball back for Ryan to toss again.

"There didn't appear to be anything missing, plus Aunt Bess and Scott wisely pointed out that there were both more convenient and more lucrative places to rob if that was the killer's intention."

He tossed the ball and then leaned back against the sofa cushions where Princess Eloise purred at his side. "Either someone with a grudge against her arrived at the lodge without knowledge of Barbara's presence and seized the opportunity, or someone specifically came to the lodge with the intent to kill her."

"Barbara did tell us all at dinner Friday night that she was recently divorced and that her husband and his *entire atmosphere* was toxic," I said. "I'd imagine the ex will be Captain Spencer's prime suspect."

"That's where I'd start."

I leaned over and kissed him. "Thankfully, it's not our problem to worry about."

And it wasn't.

Yet.

My first clue that we still hadn't been able to put our ski lodge weekend behind us was the next morning when I was in the café doing breakfast prep. Scott wasn't there, so when I heard the front door open, I assumed it was he or Luis coming inside.

"Good morning!" I called.

"Hey!"

I froze, a chill running through me. While the voice wasn't a familiar one, it was one I'd heard recently but couldn't quite place. I stepped out of the kitchen still holding the knife I'd been using to chop shallots.

"Sylvie…hi."

"This café is adorable!"

As she looked around, I saw the place as she might: a cheery blue and yellow décor, bamboo flooring, clusters of bistro tables, a long counter with round-topped stools in front of the serving window, and a display case that would soon hold the cinnamon rolls and cupcakes that I currently had baking in the oven.

"Thank you," I said. "A lot of work has gone into it, and I'm proud of it."

"You should be." She craned her neck, and I guessed she was searching for Scott.

"What brings you to the Down South Café?"

"Breakfast." She grinned. "What else? You said to come by if I was ever in town."

"I sure did. We aren't officially open yet, but if you'll give me a few minutes to finish my prep work, I can take your order."

"Sure, no problem." She took a seat at the counter. "You guys only got a dusting of snow here. It's like powdered sugar on a doughnut."

To my relief, I saw Scott's car pulling into the parking lot. The front tire on the passenger side was a spare.

Poor Scott. We might not have anywhere near as much snow as Beech Mountain, but it was still a cold, blustery morning to have to change a tire.

"Would you like coffee?" I asked Sylvie.

"Please."

After pouring hers, I filled a mug for Scott. I was certain he needed it.

He was briskly rubbing his hands together as he entered the diner.

Holding out the mug, I said, "I figured you could use this."

"Thank you." He gratefully took the steaming mug. Then he noticed our guest. "Sylvie?"

"Surprise!" She giggled. "I was in the neighborhood, so I thought I'd have breakfast at the famous Down South Café!"

"Well." He glanced from Sylvie to me. "How about that?"

"Yes, how about that? And I might stick around here for a few days!"

"That's fantastic," I said, not really believing it was fantastic but not knowing what else to say. "Where are you staying?"

"I'm staying at a hotel in Brea Ridge. So, I'm only a hop, skip, and a jump away." She blew on her coffee to cool it. "Maybe you could show me around Winter Garden while I'm here."

Although I knew she'd been addressing Scott, I answered her. "I'd love to, but there really isn't much to see. There *is* the bookstore owned by Mr. Poston. That's nice."

"It is." Scott placed his mug of coffee on the counter. "I'm going to hang up my coat and get busy. I've left you in the lurch for long enough."

"It looks as if you had to stop and change a tire," I said.

"I did. Terrible way to start the day." He threw a scowl in Sylvie's direction, and I could tell the flat tire wasn't his only nasty surprise this morning.

Like me, he was likely wondering what she was doing here in Winter Garden. It was obvious she had a crush on Scott, but he'd done nothing to encourage her attention and had let her know he was involved with someone else. Had she merely wanted to explore Winter Garden after hearing us talk about it? Or was she a stalker?

Luis walked through the door, immediately sensed the tension in the room, and looked at me. "Hey."

I smiled in an attempt to let him know everything was fine. "Good morning. Well, not so much for Scott—he had a flat tire."

"Bummer," he said.

Scott came back from hanging up his coat. "Good to see you, man."

"Sorry about your tire. I'll follow you to a garage after work if you want," Luis said.

"That would be super, you know, in case the spare blows or something."

"Scott, don't say that!" Sylvie exclaimed. "That sounds so scary."

"Luis, meet Sylvie," I said. "Scott and I met her when we were in Beech Mountain."

"What brought you all the way here?" Luis asked. "Do you have family in this area?"

"Nope." Sylvie grinned. "Scott and Amy made this place sound so charming that I had to come see it for myself."

"That's cool, I guess." The young man looked from me to Scott and back again.

"How was your weekend?" I asked him. "Did you do anything fun?"

"I went for a hike with my family. It was a little cold, but we dressed in layers and all that jazz." He rolled his eyes. "Mom insisted."

"Your mom is a smart woman. She wants to keep her family healthy."

"I know, I know," he said. "What about you two? How was the party?"

Sylvie didn't give Scott or me an opportunity to answer. "It didn't go as they expected, that's for sure! A woman was murdered in the kitchen of the ski lodge. Isn't that the wildest?"

"Yeah, well, too bad we don't have time to discuss that right now," I said. "We need to finish our prep work because other customers will be coming in soon. On that note, Sylvie, what are you having for breakfast?"

"I'll take some bacon and eggs and—" She sniffed. "Do I smell cinnamon rolls?"

"There are some in the oven, yes."

"One of those too, please," she said.

As if on cue, the oven timer buzzed.

"I'll take care of that," Scott said, as he hurried into the kitchen.

Before I could join him, Dilly and Walter arrived.

"Amy!" Dilly grabbed me in a bear hug with a strength that belied her looks. "I've missed you these past few days!"

"I've missed you too. How's Buddy?" Buddy was the raccoon who came down out of the woods to Dilly's back porch every evening for a biscuit. "Mom made sure he had his biscuit, didn't she?"

"Well, of course, she did. But she didn't put peanut butter on it like *some* people." Dilly arched her brows at me.

I laughed. "What will you two be having for breakfast this morning?"

"If she hasn't changed her mind, my beloved will be having the Belgian waffles," Walter said. "I'd like a southwestern omelet."

"Coming right up."

"I want to hear all about your big weekend!" Dilly called as I went into the kitchen. "From you too, Scott!"

After pouring coffee for the patrons, I went into the kitchen where Scott was already plating Sylvie's bacon, eggs, and cinnamon roll.

"Will you take this out to her?" he asked. "What is she *doing* here? Do you think she's here because of *me*? I made it as clear to her as I could that I'm seeing someone. What if Leslie should come by and see Sylvie here? She'll think I did something to encourage Sylvie."

Placing my hand on his arm, I said, "No, she won't. It'll be fine. If Leslie has any questions, I'll help you explain the situation to her." I took the plate. "Would you mind starting on Dilly's waffles? I'll work on Walter's omelet as soon as I return from delivering this to Sylvie."

"Let's hope she eats it and leaves quickly."

I nodded, but I didn't hold my breath. Sylvie didn't come all this way to eat breakfast and then return to Beech Mountain.

By the time I walked from the kitchen to the dining room with Sylvie's plate, she was already telling Walter and Dilly all about what a fiasco the grand opening party turned into after Barbara Hayter was found dead in the fridge.

"I met a realtor named Barbara Hayter at a benefit for a children's charity a few years ago," Dilly said.

"Barbara was a realtor," Sylvie said.

"If it's the same woman, that's a shame." Dilly blushed. "I mean, it's a shame no matter who it was, but the woman I met seemed really nice. Although come to think of it, her husband was obnoxious."

"Barbara and her husband recently got divorced." Sylvie paused her conversation only long enough to mutter thanks when I sat the plate in front of her. "My cousin is a law enforcement officer, and he told me they went looking for the ex because of course he was their number one suspect, but he's currently out of the country and has been for two weeks."

"That doesn't mean he wasn't behind the murder," Walter said.

"I agree." Dilly nodded. "He could've hired someone to do the deed and left the country to establish his alibi."

"My lovely wife and I watch a lot of true crime television." Walter winked at Dilly, and she blushed.

I was thinking about their conversation as I returned to the kitchen. If Barbara's ex-husband *did* hire the murderer, that was horrible. The thought of one of the guests being a professional assassin was truly frightening.

But was it any less scary to think that one of the guests was an amateur who acted alone?

# Chapter Seven

Sylvie hung around for far too long, but thankfully, she'd left by the time Homer Pickens came in for his sausage biscuit. Homer was a regular who liked to have his sausage biscuit and coffee at ten-thirty every morning. And each day, Homer had a new hero and wise words to offer from that particular hero. Since Scott and I had been away, I shouldn't have been surprised to learn that Homer's hero of the day was Ibn Battuta, the famous traveler.

"Welcome home," Homer said, as he took his usual seat at the counter. "Ibn Battuta said that traveling leaves you speechless and then turns you into a storyteller. Did you bring home any stories?"

"I'm afraid we did." I poured him a cup of medium roast coffee.

The breakfast rush was over, and there were only a couple of other patrons in the café, so both Scott and I had a moment to linger and chat with Homer.

Scott took out his phone and showed Homer a photograph of the cake he'd made for the grand opening of the ski lodge. "I made the cake to showcase the legend of some Civil War gold that's supposed to be in a cave somewhere near the lodge. The bear is because the name of the lodge is *Yona*, which is the Cherokee word for *bear*."

Homer gave a low whistle. "That's some cake. I imagine the people at the lodge were truly impressed and honored to have such an incredible cake."

"I suppose, but the whole event was overshadowed by a murder that occurred prior to the start of the party."

"A murder? What happened?"

Scott told him the whole story.

"Was the murderer caught?" Homer asked.

"Not as of the time that we left," I said. "Scott and I were a little nervous that the police captain suspected us of the crime because the woman was hit on the head with a cast-iron skillet."

"Oh, that's ridiculous." Homer sipped his coffee. "The only thing that cast-iron skillet tells us is that the murder was unplanned."

I considered his statement. "You know what? You're right. I hadn't thought of that."

Should I have been concerned that so many of my favorite customers were true crime aficionados? Maybe. But they sure were smart.

Nevertheless, Barbara Hayter's murder was none of my business. It was a matter for the Beech Mountain police to solve.

Still, I couldn't help but wonder who among the guests could have had a grudge against Barbara. None of the attendees at dinner on Friday night seemed to have been acquainted with her until then.

The rest of the day was busy but nothing we couldn't handle. Jackie came in after her class. At the end of the day when we were cleaning up, we told her about our unexpected visitor. She agreed with Scott and me that Sylvie coming all the way to Winter Garden was weird.

"If she comes back while I'm here, I'll send her packing," she said.

"I don't want to hurt her feelings—or our business," I said. "She didn't do anything wrong."

"Other than stalk *me*," Scott added.

"She can't help herself," Luis teased. "You're a catch, bro."

"Truer words were never spoken, dude." Scott laughed and helped Luis put the chairs atop the tables so we could mop the floor.

"Looks like Sylvie isn't going to be our only unexpected Beech Mountain visitor today," I said.

Everyone else followed my gaze to the parking lot where a police cruiser was parking.

"Who's that?" Jackie stormed over to the front door.

I said nothing, but my heart was pounding in my throat as Captain Spencer got out of the car. All I could think was that Scott or I—maybe both of us—was about to be arrested, and neither of us had done anything wrong.

Jackie opened the door before Captain Spencer even got to it. "We're closed."

"Are Scott and Amy here?" he asked.

"You know they are. You're looking right at them." She still didn't move out of the doorway to allow Captain Spencer to come inside. Her brash temperament came from Aunt Bess's side of the family.

"It's all right, Jackie," I said.

"Amy, I'd like to speak with you and Scott please." Captain Spencer narrowed his eyes at Jackie. "Alone, if at all possible."

"We can sit at this table in the corner," I said.

"But we'd like to get home today." Jackie reluctantly moved away from the door. "And the rest of the staff is going to continue cleaning up so we can leave."

"Fine." Captain Spencer moved to the table I'd indicated.

"Would you like a cup of coffee?" I asked.

"No, thank you." He nodded toward the other chairs.

Scott and I joined Captain Spencer at the table.

"What are you doing here?" I asked. "I believed Scott and I were cleared yesterday morning when you said we could return home."

"I told the two of you that you were free to go but that I might have additional questions." He looked from me to Scott.

Even though it felt as if he was trying to intimidate us, I thought it was a good sign that he was willing to question us together. Also, it was nice that he didn't insist on having us return to Beech Mountain. Could he do that? I had no idea, but I supposed it didn't really matter at this point.

"Are you sure you wouldn't like to have a cup of coffee?" Jackie asked. "Even though it's the end of the day, I'd be happy to make you a fresh pot."

"Would you now? Wonder why I find that thought so disturbing?" Captain Spencer asked.

"Aw, I promise not to spit in it. I'll even have a cup too if it would make you feel better." Jackie gave him a broad smile. "I feel like I didn't make a great first impression on you, and that reflects badly on the Down South Café."

"I really don't need any coffee, but thank you," he said.

"How about a soda?" she asked. "That wouldn't be any trouble at all. No dirty dishes to clean up or anything."

Scott and I shared a side glance. Jackie was up to something—we just didn't know what.

It didn't take long to realize why she'd been stalling the captain.

Sheriff Billings' police cruiser rolled practically to the door of the café, and it seemed as if the engine hadn't even quit before the sheriff, Ryan, and Ivy stormed into the café. I focused my eyes on the tabletop to keep from laughing.

"Well, Ms. Flowers, it appears you've called in the cavalry," Captain Spencer said. "Did you believe that to be necessary?"

"No, sir. I didn't call anyone."

"Sure you won't have that soda?" Jackie asked, with a self-satisfied smirk.

"I'm fine." He glared at her.

"Actually, if I *was* going to call someone," I said, "it would have been Aunt Bess. She was terribly disappointed when she had to leave the lodge and could no longer take part in the investigation."

"I'd like to know what's going on here," Sheriff Billings said. "You've come a long way to have a chat. Are you accusing either of these people of anything?"

"I'm not. However, it often does me good and helps me put matters into perspective when I get out of the office."

"It does me, too, but it usually doesn't take me two hours of driving to clear my head."

"My head *is* clear, Sheriff, but I'm dealing with a murder that isn't easily solved. Would you like to sit in while I interview these two witnesses again?"

"Absolutely."

Sheriff Billings, Ryan, and Ivy took a seat at the table next to the one where Scott and I sat with Captain Spencer.

Judging by the grim expression on his face, Captain Spencer didn't appreciate the audience, but there wasn't much he could do about it. "Were any of the guests showing any animosity toward Barbara Hayter on Friday evening?"

"Not only did no one show her any animosity, no one showed anyone else any emotion other than polite detachment," I said. "Friday was an awkward meeting of people who didn't know each other and had little, if any, prior connection. For instance, I'd met Katherine and Bill Donahue only once briefly when they passed through Winter Garden and ate at the café, which is why they said they called to ask me to cater their party when their own chef became unavailable."

Captain Spencer addressed Scott. "What about you?"

"The only people there that I knew were Amy and Aunt Bess."

"And did you see or hear anything suspicious?" Captain Spencer asked.

Scott's lips twitched.

"Do you find something funny, young man?"

Ivy tensed.

"I'm sorry," Scott said. "I'm just thinking about what Aunt Bess would say, and she'd tell you that the most suspicious thing we saw was Barbara eating that head of lettuce."

"I'm well aware of that." Captain Spencer rolled his eyes. "Your aunt made that abundantly clear to me."

"Maybe there was something to that lettuce thing," Jackie said. "Maybe Barbara knew someone was after her and was afraid to eat something with strong flavors like a pizza because the taste of poison could have been disguised."

Turning to look at Jackie, I said, "Oh, my gosh! You have a point!"

Captain Spencer gave a deep sigh. "We don't have a lot of murders to solve in Beech Mountain."

I took pity on him. "I understand, Captain. Plus, according to Sylvie, who also came to Winter Garden to see us today, Barbara's husband has an ironclad alibi. And even if he didn't, it's apparent from the choice of weapon that the attack on Barbara wasn't premeditated."

His jaw went slack. "What the—?"

"As you can see, you aren't dealing with amateurs here, Captain," Sheriff Billings said. "We, unfortunately, have had more than our fair share of homicides in Winter Garden."

"That would explain *your* expertise, but *she* works in a café." Captain Spencer looked as if he was reconsidering that offer of a soda or coffee.

"Amy doesn't simply *work* in this café," Ryan said, "she *owns* it. We don't underestimate people around here."

"That wasn't my intention." He looked at me. "I apologize, Amy."

"Accepted." I started to add that I thought he should widen his focus to other people who knew Barbara—her coworkers, her family, her friends; but I thought that not only was he probably already doing that, but that I should keep my mouth shut. I seldom ever knew to quit when I was ahead. This time I did.

# Chapter Eight

After Captain Spencer left, I returned the van to the rental place and was delighted to have my Bug back. Nana had bought me the yellow Volkswagen Beetle brand new when I'd graduated from high school. It had quite a few miles on it now, but it still ran well, and the thought of trading it for another vehicle made me feel sad. While the van had been luxurious and had many figurative bells and whistles that my car lacked, I wouldn't take it over my little Bug.

Driving toward home, I wondered exactly what Sylvie had hoped to gain by coming to Winter Garden. Had she thought to show her devotion to Scott by following him here even after he'd told her he was involved with someone else? If so, how crazy was that? She didn't even know Scott.

Furthermore, what had prompted Captain Spencer to drive all the way here to question Scott and me for less than an hour? He'd spent half his day doing something he could have done much quicker by phone or video chat.

Even though Captain Spencer had said the drive helped to clear his head, Sheriff Billings was spot on when he'd observed that he usually didn't have to drive two hours to gain clarity. Captain Spencer had driven four hours counting his return trip to Beech Mountain.

It occurred to me that perhaps Captain Spencer didn't return home, that it was possible he'd stayed in Brea Ridge or Abingdon. But if so, why would he do that? Had Barbara Hayter had ties to Winter Garden that Captain Spencer was keeping to himself?

As I drove, I forced myself to put Barbara's murder and all the crazy things surrounding it out of my head. Jackie and I had decided not to inform Aunt Bess that Captain Spencer had paid a visit to the Down South Café. It was better for all of us to keep that bit of information to ourselves. I could tell, though, that it pained Jackie not to be able to share her theory of Barbara's fear of being poisoned being the reason she ate the head of lettuce. Still, we didn't want to have to return with Aunt Bess to Beech Mountain because Scott and I had gotten to speak with Captain Spencer again and she hadn't.

I swung back by the café to pick up the chicken casserole and slices of pumpkin cheesecake I'd put aside for Mom and Aunt Bess. Turning into the parking lot, I was surprised to see a black SUV with Georgia tags.

Making sure my doors were locked, I pulled up beside the other vehicle. Jackie's boyfriend, Roger, had installed a wonderful security system outside the café, and I should have probably driven on by and called to have the police investigate the trespasser. But while I had no intention of getting out of my car and confronting anyone, I did want the person or persons to know I was aware of their presence.

I hoped they also knew I was calling the sheriff's office. I was fumbling in my purse for my phone when Professor Goodwin got out of the driver's side of the SUV. He was smiling as he approached my car, but I still didn't quite trust him.

Putting my window down about a quarter of an inch, I said, "This is a surprise."

"I hope it's a pleasant one." He didn't give me an opportunity to either confirm or deny his statement. "I was about to leave you a note, but I feared it would get ruined or lost if I left it on the door. I'm glad you're here now."

"The café is closed for the day."

"Oh, no. You misunderstand." He raised his gloved hands. "As much as I am looking forward to partaking in more of your fabulous cuisine, I'm actually in town hoping to speak with Scott."

"Is that so?"

"Yes. I'm interested in the research of Beech Mountain he did for his cake." He gazed at me expectantly.

"I'm not comfortable giving out Scott's phone number without his permission," I said. "You may either give me your information to pass along to him, or you may come by the café during regular hours and speak with him then."

"All right." He produced a business card from his jacket pocket and poked it through the small opening in the window. "Would you please ask him to call me?"

I took the card. "I'll pass along your message."

"Thank you. Have a pleasant evening." He strode back to the SUV and got inside.

I waited until he'd driven away before I got out of my car, let myself into the café, and locked the door behind me. Sure, I was only going to be a minute, but I wasn't taking any chances. What in the world did this history professor want to speak with Scott about?

When I got to the big house, I stepped into the kitchen and turned on the oven to warm the casserole. Mom and Aunt Bess must have been in another part of the house because they didn't greet me when I came in.

While I was waiting for the oven to pre-heat, I went back outside and called Scott.

"Hey, Amy-girl, what's up?"

"I stopped by the café to pick up dinner for Mom and Aunt Bess, and Professor Goodwin was there. He wants to talk with you."

"About what?" Scott's frustration was evident in his voice.

Who could blame him? First, Sylvie and now the professor. It was downright bizarre.

"He said he wanted to speak with you about the research you did for your cake design," I said. "I told him I didn't feel comfortable giving him your phone number but that I'd pass along his information to you."

"Thanks. I appreciate that."

"So, do you want the professor's phone number?"

"No." He paused. "Is that mean of me? I've got plans with Leslie this evening, and I feel like I've been interrogated enough over the past couple of days. Besides, I don't want some stranger having my personal number—which he will if I call him."

"I don't blame you a bit. I'm simply passing along the message because I told him I would."

"I know." Scott sighed. "Maybe I'll feel more accommodating tomorrow and will call him from the café's landline during a break."

"All right. It wouldn't surprise me, though, if he didn't come by the café tomorrow."

"If he was so all-fired interested in my research, why didn't he speak with me about it while we were still at the lodge?" he asked.

"I don't know. Maybe if you get a chance to speak with him, you can ask him." I decided to confess my misgivings. "I was more than a little freaked out when I saw an SUV with Georgia tags parked in front of the café. Even after I saw that it was Professor Goodwin, I stayed in my car with the doors locked and the driver's side window lowered only enough for him to be able to hand me his card."

"Have you told Ryan about the professor hanging out at the café like some creep lying in wait?"

"Not yet." I felt as if maybe I was being unfair to the professor. "I don't know how long he'd been there. To be fair, he might've just arrived when I drove up."

"Maybe. Still, I feel like Ryan needs to be aware of the situation."

"True. I'll tell him later this evening."

We said our goodbyes, and I went into the kitchen to see that the oven had preheated and that Mom had already put in the casserole.

"Thanks," I said.

"Thank you. After all, it's our dinner. Why did you go outside to use your phone? What's going on?"

Shrugging, I said, "Nothing. No reason."

"I know better." She made that you-might-as-well-tell-me Mom look.

"It's been a strange day, that's all."

"Strange how?" Aunt Bess asked as she strolled into the kitchen and took a seat at the table. "Come on. Pull out a chair and spill the tea. That's what the kids call spilling your guts these days, Jenna."

Mom nodded. "Aunt Bess is right. Sit down and talk to us."

I still wasn't about to tell Aunt Bess about Captain Spencer being at the café, but I didn't think it would hurt to tell her and Mom about Sylvie and Professor Goodwin. So, I did.

"Why would these two strangers drive all the way to Winter Garden?" I asked when I'd concluded my abridged account of the day.

"Sylvie has a crush on Scott," Aunt Bess said. "I'm not surprised she came chasing after him."

"But he let her know he wasn't interested and that he was dating someone else," I said.

"Knowing a person is unavailable makes them all the more attractive to some people." Aunt Bess opened the box with the cheesecake and took out a slice. "Jenna, you're closer to the silverware drawer; get me a fork, would you?"

Mom looked as if she were debating whether or not to chide Aunt Bess for eating dessert before dinner. After a moment, she simply got up and retrieved three forks. She handed one fork to Aunt Bess and one to me. She then took out the other slice of cheesecake and placed it between the two of us.

"I agree with Scott about the professor," Mom said, cutting into the cheesecake with her fork. "Why didn't the professor talk with Scott while you were all still at the lodge? Especially if he drove from Georgia to be at the lodge to begin with. He drove all this extra way to come here." She took a bite of the cheesecake. "Mmm. This is delicious, honey."

"Yes, it is," Aunt Bess said, already halfway through hers. "I love pumpkin. As for the professor, maybe he just didn't want to go home after the police closed down the lodge."

"Then why not take a room at another resort?" I asked.

"Good question." Aunt Bess shook her fork. "I'll ask him tomorrow."

"Tomorrow?" I shared a panicked look with Mom.

Aunt Bess nodded as she dug back into her slice of cheesecake. "I plan to be there early and stay as late as I have to in order to ask that man what he's up to."

"But he might not even show up," I said.

"Amy's got a point. He could've merely been passing through."

"Nah," Aunt Bess said. "He'll be there."

Mom tried again. "What will you do all day? You'll be bored to tears."

"Not me. I'll bring a book." She nodded. "Be ready by six, Jenna."

Fortunately, the oven timer went off and brought an end to that conversation.

# Chapter Nine

I felt slightly apprehensive when I arrived at work Tuesday morning. Although I'd been able to put Monday's events out of my mind for the most part last night with a fun evening spent at home with Ryan, Rory, and Princess Eloise—whose second favorite person in the world is Ryan, by the way—I dreaded what today would bring. I knew the Bible said for us to be anxious for nothing, but that was so much easier said than done.

I let out a breath of relief when Scott pulled into the parking lot beside me.

"I'm so glad you're here," I said, as we both got out of our cars. "And I see that you have a new tire."

He nodded. "There was no fixing the old one. How are you this morning?"

I started to give the glib answer cold, but he knew me too well. Besides, I imagined he was even more concerned than I was since he was the one the Beech Mountain people were coming to see.

"Honestly, I'm nervous. Sylvie being here was odd, but I can see how impetuous she is and that she has a crush on you." I sighed, and my breath emerged as condensation in the cold air. "The professor being here is even more weird."

"I agree." He jerked his chin toward the door. "Let's get inside where it's warm, and we'll talk while we do breakfast prep."

Nodding, I hurried to the door and unlocked it. This morning, we locked the door behind us. As soon as we put our coats away, I made our usual three pots of coffee—medium roast, French vanilla, and decaf. Soon, the rich aroma of brewing coffee filled the café.

I poured myself a cup of French vanilla and Scott a cup of medium roast and took the cups into the kitchen where Scott was already mixing up a batch of brownies.

"Thanks," he said. "Leslie and I were talking about the professor last night. Why would a history professor be interested in the research of a layperson—her word, not mine?"

Suppressing a grin, I silently acknowledged that Scott wasn't the type to use the word *layperson* as I scooped some flour out of an airtight plastic bin and dumped it into a mixing bowl. "That's true. You can't tell me a history professor wouldn't have access to the same information you found."

"Exactly." He spread the brownie batter into a pan and placed it in the pre-heated oven. "The dude has access to way more resources than I did. Why does he care about my research? I learned enough about a local legend to create an interesting cake."

"An incredible cake," I said. "And if he was a wannabe cake artist, I'd completely understand why he'd want to talk with you about how you created the cake."

"Right?" He took the mixing bowl over to the sink to wash it rather than put it in the dishwasher. It was his favorite bowl, and he wanted to use it again. "Leslie made that point, too. I was flattered that she thought the cake was that impressive."

"You've got to stop underestimating yourself." I added the rest of the biscuit ingredients to the flour.

"Good morning!" Luis called.

"Hi, Luis!" I answered. "Did you lock the door back?"

"Yes!" After hanging up his coat, he came into the kitchen. "What's going on? I thought it was weird that you guys had locked the door behind you. Is there an escaped convict or something?"

I explained about the professor.

"We don't trust his explanation for why he's here," Scott said. "It doesn't make sense."

Luis shook his head. "No more out-of-town catering gigs for you two. You get into too much trouble."

Not ten minutes after we opened for business, in waltzed a chipper Aunt Bess. She was followed by a groggy Mom, who immediately requested a pot of coffee with one cream and two sugars.

Laughing, I said, "I believe you mean a *cup* of coffee."

"I said what I meant." She dragged herself over to a table near the counter, pulled out a chair, and dropped onto it.

"Okaaay. I'll bring you that pot a cup at a time, all right?"

Her only response was the bobbing of her head, which either meant *yes* or that she was nodding off.

"Good morning, sunshine," Scott said to Aunt Bess as he came out of the kitchen.

"Good morning, darlin'. Now, don't you worry one iota about that little hussy or that weirdo. Your Aunt Bess is here to keep 'em in line."

He gave her a hug. "You're the best."

"I know." She perched on a stool at the counter. "What good stuff have you got made for breakfast?"

I sat Mom's coffee in front of her. Her eyes were closed, and I thought she'd possibly dozed off. I walked away quietly, not wanting to disturb her any more than she already was.

"Aunt Bess, would you like regular or French vanilla coffee?" I asked.

"Let's go with that French vanilla." She wriggled her shoulders. "I feel an *ooh, la la* coming on. And in keeping with the theme, I'd like an order of French toast with a side of *la bacon*."

Dilly and Walter arrived in time to hear Aunt Bess's order.

"French toast and bacon sound good to me," Dilly said. "Make it two please, Amy."

"Just make it three while you're at it," Walter said.

"Bess, it's a pleasure to see you this morning." Dilly took a seat at her usual table, which was close enough to the counter that she could carry on a conversation with Aunt Bess. "How have you been?"

As Walter sat down by his wife, Aunt Bess launched into her explanation of what she was doing at the café at the break of day. I gratefully retreated to the kitchen to prepare French toast and bacon. *Ooh, la la* indeed.

By the time the morning rush was in full swing, Mom had left after instructing Aunt Bess to call her when she was ready to go home. So far, Aunt Bess hadn't shown any signs of winding down. She'd chatted with patrons, kept an eye on the door, and hadn't even opened the book she'd brought—Ann Rule's *The Stranger Beside Me*.

I overheard Luis ask her about the book.

"Oh, yes, it's an interesting read," she replied. "I'll let you borrow it at the end of the day. Right now, I need it to show certain people that I am well versed in psychopaths and that I'm not to be trifled with."

"Thanks." He finished bussing a nearby table.

When Homer came in that morning, he appeared to be delighted to see Aunt Bess. Of course, the breakfast rush had passed, and the lunch rush hadn't started. There was only one empty seat at the counter between Homer's usual seat and the stool on which Aunt Bess sat, so they could chat comfortably.

As I poured Homer's coffee, I gave him a cheery *good morning* and asked who his hero was today.

"Yay!" Aunt Bess clapped her hands. "I usually ask Amy about your heroes, Homer, but today I'll get to hear everything firsthand."

I topped off Aunt Bess's glass of water. I'd suspended her coffee consumption hours ago.

"My hero today is the talented actor, Alan Alda, who once said, 'You have to leave the city of your comfort and go into the wilderness of your intuition. What you'll discover will be wonderful. What you'll discover is yourself.'"

"Well, how nice," Aunt Bess said. "Wasn't that lovely, Amy?" Before I could confirm that Homer's quote was lovely, she continued. "That's what I'm doing today. I left the comfort of my home to go into the wilderness of the Down South Café to protect my loved ones from rascals and hooligans."

Managing to refrain from rolling my eyes and giving Homer a smile, I said, "Be right back with your sausage biscuit."

Homer and Aunt Bess were happily discussing rascals, hooligans, and Alan Alda's performances when I went into the kitchen.

"How long do you think Aunt Bess intends to stay?" Scott asked me quietly.

"I have no idea. I'm frankly surprised she's stayed this long." I put Homer's sausage patty on the grill.

"No chance of me slipping her out the back and taking her home?"

"I highly doubt it. You know she's as stubborn as the day is long. It wouldn't shock me if she stayed right there on that stool until she saw the hussy or the weirdo." I laughed. "Let's hope she'll be disappointed."

"I don't think she will be." He nodded toward the window, and I moved over so I could see what he was talking about.

Captain Spencer was striding across the parking lot toward the door. Behind him were Katherine and Bill Donahue.

"No." I blinked a few times, wishing the trio would be a hallucination that Scott and I were somehow sharing. Sadly, they were not.

As I stood rooted to the spot, Scott had the presence of mind to flip Homer's sausage patty before it burned.

"Thank you." I turned back to the grill.

"You take care of Homer," he said, "and I'll go see what our guests would like to order."

"What are y'all doing here?" I heard Aunt Bess's voice above the sizzle of the sausage.

Scott greeted our guests, but I couldn't make out their conversation beyond that. Either my heart pounding in my ears or the popping of the grease drowned out the noise around me. Even the soft jazz music we had playing faded into the background.

Deep down, I knew I had no reason to be so rattled. I'd done nothing wrong, and neither had Scott or Aunt Bess. Why, then, were all these people from the ski lodge converging on the Down South Café?

As I was taking Homer his biscuit, Jackie—who had the day off because she was supposed to be in classes all day—marched into the café.

"Granny, Aunt Jenna told me you were here and that you have been all morning. What in the world are you doing?"

"I'm here making sure these rascals—" She gestured toward the table where Captain Spencer, Katherine, and Bill sat. "—and the hussy and the weirdo stay in line."

Katherine laughed. "You are such a delight."

I sat the plate in front of Homer and refilled his coffee cup. Whispering, I asked, "Does Alan Alda have any words of wisdom that might apply to this situation?"

"Not that I know of," he answered. "And neither do I."

# Chapter Ten

Jackie tried to convince Aunt Bess to allow her to drive her home. "I need to get back to class, Granny, and I can't see any peace if I'm worrying about you."

"What do you think is going to happen to me here in your cousin's café?" Aunt Bess asked. "Are you afraid I'm gonna starve to death? Captain Spencer has come all this way to take me up on my offer to help him. I can't just turn my back on the man."

"Um…actually, I would like to speak with you if it wouldn't be too much trouble," Captain Spencer said.

"I thought you'd already taken Granny's statement at the ski lodge on Sunday." Jackie glared at the captain.

"And that's when I told him to let me know if he needed my help." Aunt Bess spread her hands. "Obviously, he does."

Katherine and Bill were watching this exchange with bemused smiles on their faces.

"Would anyone like a menu?" I asked.

Frankly, I didn't know why Jackie was making such a big deal of Aunt Bess being here, either. It wasn't like I'd let anything bad happen to her. Furthermore, this was a place of business—my place of business—not a three-ring circus.

"I'd love a menu," Katherine said.

"I imagine you're wondering what we're doing here." Bill took the menus I offered him and handed one to his wife. "After Barbara's death, all our guests either canceled their reservations or rescheduled."

"We can only hope they'll reschedule." Katherine's smile had been replaced by a worried frown. "We desperately needed something to cheer us up, and we thought a day trip to Winter Garden might do the trick."

"Say, Scott, you couldn't draw us a map to where that Civil War gold is buried, could you?" Bill laughed as if he'd told the funniest joke anyone had ever heard.

No one else even chuckled.

"I'm sorry, sir," Scott said. "I sure wish I could."

"You know, my granddaughter, Jackie, made an excellent observation about Barbara," Aunt Bess said.

"It's possible she ate that head of lettuce Friday night because she was afraid of being poisoned. Now, I personally believe it was awfully rude of her to book a reservation from you during your grand opening weekend if she suspected there was a killer after her, but there you go."

"I don't think Barbara feared for her life," Katherine said. "If so, she never mentioned it. Besides, we ordered out that evening, and we all ate the same things."

"She was our realtor when we bought the land for the ski lodge, and we became quite friendly with her." Bill put aside his menu. "I should hope she'd have told us—or someone—if she felt her life was in danger."

"None of us—and by us, I mean Granny, Scott, and Amy—knew this Barbara Hayter or had any desire to harm her," Jackie said. "So, why are you here, Captain Spencer? And why are Sylvie and Professor Goodwin here?"

"Sylvie and Charles are here?" Bill asked.

"They were both here yesterday, but I haven't seen either of them today." Glancing outside, I saw two cars pulling into the parking lot and knew more would be arriving soon. "Captain Spencer, if you do have questions for Aunt Bess, Scott, and me, I respectfully request that you wait to talk with us until after we close the café for the day."

"That's at three o'clock," Scott added.

"That works for me," Jackie said. "Granny, I can take you home now and bring you back at three, if that works for the two of you."

"That's fine with me," Captain Spencer said. "I'm actually here for lunch."

"Could we return at that time as well?" Katherine asked. "If someone knows something that could help us get this matter laid to rest, I'd appreciate being part of that discussion."

"Okay." Captain Spencer gave an authoritative nod. "Let's plan to meet here at three. And may I please have a club sandwich with fries?"

Jackie took Aunt Bess home, and Katherine and Bill lingered over their coffee until the lunch rush finally convinced them to go explore historic Abingdon.

Then, at approximately one o'clock, Professor Goodwin showed up.

"Good afternoon!"

When I heard the booming voice, I peeped through the service window to see who it was. Then seeing who it was, I went back to cooking.

"Welcome to the Down South Café," Scott said. "Please have a seat, and I'll be with you in a moment."

Curiosity won out, and after I'd plated the dish I'd been preparing, I went into the dining room. After delivering the meal to the customer, I spoke to Professor Goodwin.

"Hello. Nice to see you again."

"You, too, Amy."

"May I take your order?"

He shook his head. "That's all right. I'll wait for Scott."

Scott joined us then. "May *I* take your order?"

"Yes, but first, I'd like to hear about your research into—"

"Not to be rude," Scott interrupted, "but I'm working and don't have time to chat right now. If you'd like to come back at three p.m., I'll be happy to talk with you then."

"Very well." Professor Goodwin took the menu Scott offered and perused it. "I'd like a chef's salad then."

"Good choice," I said. "I'll get that started for you."

When Scott came into the kitchen a few minutes later, I said quietly, "That was a wise approach to the professor. Let him explain to you *and* Captain Spencer what he's doing here."

"I'm more than a pretty face, you know." He grinned.

"Absolutely. I've got to admit, I'm still confused as to why Captain Spencer is here when Barbara's murder occurred in Beech Mountain."

"Me, too. Let's just hope we don't have to deal with Sylvie anymore." He went back out into the dining room, leaving me to shred lettuce and chop spinach for Professor Goodwin's salad.

"Hey, Scott!"

Hearing Ryan's voice made me smile as my shoulders relaxed.

After greeting Ryan, Scott came into the kitchen. "Let me finish making that salad while you go out and take Ryan's order."

"Thanks. You're the best."

"I know."

I laughed. "You've been hanging out with Aunt Bess too much."

Ryan smiled when he saw me. "Hello, beautiful."

"Hi, handsome. What would you like for lunch?"

"A burger and fries would be great," he said. "Are we still on for the movies tonight?"

"You bet." Aware that Professor Goodwin was probably listening to our conversation, I bent and whispered in Ryan's ear. "Captain Spencer will be back here at three. Several other people will be too in case you're interested."

"Oh, I'm interested," he said softly.

Smiling, I poured him a glass of iced tea. "I'll go make that burger."

"Thanks, sweetheart."

Scott passed me with Professor Goodwin's salad on my way back to the kitchen. "Getting awfully chummy with thc customers, aren't you?"

"You know it," I said lightly, but I still blushed at his teasing.

He stopped suddenly. "You've gotta be kidding me."

"What is it?" I turned and followed his gaze.

Doug, his wife, and his daughter were walking into the café.

"Professor Goodwin, what a surprise to see you here!" Doug raised his hand in a friendly wave. "Hey, Scott…Amy! Professor, do you care if we join you?"

"Not at all." The professor looked as if he *did* care but was too polite to say so.

"Nice to see you all," I said. "I need to get back into the kitchen."

"Yeah, we'll talk with you soon," Doug said. "We were visiting relatives in Brea Ridge and thought that since we were this close, we'd pop in and have some more of that delicious Down South Café food."

I returned to the kitchen, relieved to have work to do and somewhere to hide. I'd have asked myself if this day could get any weirder, but I was afraid the day would tell me to hold its beer.

# Chapter Eleven

The day sped right along, and three o'clock arrived almost before I knew what was happening. Nearly in perfect sync with my flipping the café sign from *Open* to *Closed*, Captain Spencer, Professor Goodwin, Katherine, Bill, Jackie, Aunt Bess, Ryan, Ivy, and Sheriff Billings showed up.

"What's all this?" Professor Goodwin stood in the center of the dining room and slowly turned in a circle, arms akimbo, as he took in the other arrivals. "Am I being arrested for my curiosity? I had no idea being inquisitive was a crime."

"Relax, Goodwin. No one is being arrested," Captain Spencer said. "I'm not even sure why you're here."

"Everyone wanted to talk," I said. "Since we couldn't very well do that and operate a business, we're all here now."

"Come along, Captain." Aunt Bess sat at a table and patted the seat of the chair next to hers. "You and I can answer everyone's questions from here."

Grinning and smug in the knowledge that he wasn't the law enforcement officer in Aunt Bess's crosshairs today, Sheriff Billings asked, "Amy, have you got any leftover pie? I'll eat it from a to-go box with a plastic fork so as not to make any mess."

"Sure. We have pumpkin, coconut cream, and Boston cream."

"I'll have the coconut cream, please," he said.

"Anyone else?" I asked.

Although Ryan and Captain Spencer seemed tempted, everyone else declined. I was surprised Aunt Bess didn't want anything given her love of sweets, but I supposed she was being professional until the interrogations were concluded.

I walked over to the display case, but Luis had already put Sheriff Billings' slice of pie on a paper plate. He handed me the plate, a to-go packet containing plasticware and a napkin, and some coffee he'd poured into a lidded cup.

"I'll clean the coffee pots, but then I need to go pick up my sister from school if that's okay," he said.

"That's fine…although I'd be happy to go in your place if you'd like to hang around here."

Chuckling, he said softly, "Staying here might be fun, but I don't know. This is such a weird crowd."

"You're telling me." I delivered the pie and coffee to Sheriff Billings.

"Thanks, Amy."

By now everyone had taken a seat around the front part of the dining area. As they had done yesterday, Sheriff Billings, Ryan, and Ivy were sitting together at the table closest to Captain Spencer. Scott and I sat on stools at the counter, and Jackie perched on a chair next to Aunt Bess. For some reason, I was surprised when Katherine and Bill didn't sit with Professor Goodwin, who was at a table by himself.

I was guessing the only reason the professor didn't leave was because he was afraid it would make him look suspicious. His lips were tightly clamped together as if he had no intention of speaking except if he were tortured; and even then, it was iffy.

"I thank you all for taking time out of your busy schedule to be here," Captain Spencer said. "Especially those of you I didn't anticipate seeing again."

The captain did an excellent job of looking at no one in particular when he said that last part, but everyone could likely guess about whom he was speaking. In all the police shows I'd seen, no one group of law enforcement officers ever welcomed the interference of another group.

"I actually had no intention of rehashing the events of Sunday morning," he continued. "I truly did come into the café earlier today for a sandwich. But since Bess offered her expertise, how could I refuse?"

Aunt Bess patted his hand, gave him a wink, and decided to take over. "Thank you, Captain Spencer. I feel it would be best to begin by asking those present who were also at the ski lodge how they felt about the victim."

Sheriff Billings began coughing and spewed a mouthful of coffee onto the table. So much for his not making a mess.

Ryan patted the sheriff on the back to aid his recovery as I hurried to get paper towels and disinfectant to clean the table. Scott provided extra napkins so the sheriff could wipe the tears streaming down his face.

"Sorry," Sheriff Billings said, his voice emerging as a croak. He cleared his throat. "Please carry on."

When Scott and I had retaken our seats, Aunt Bess said, "I'll start. I have nothing to hide. I met Barbara Hayter for the first time on Friday evening and thought she was a kook. Katherine and Bill had ordered delicious pizzas, and Barbara ate a head of lettuce. From what I could see, this lettuce had nary a drop of salad dressing or seasoning of any sort on it. That was the only time I had any conversation with Barbara whatsoever, and I didn't kill her. Professor Goodwin, what's your story?"

As the rest of us turned in his direction, Professor Goodwin's face flushed. "I don't have one."

"Of course, you do," Aunt Bess said. "Tell us what you know about Barbara Hayter."

"I've given my statement to the police." He crossed his arms. "I will not be interrogated by a doddering old lady."

Jackie rose to her feet so quickly that her chair nearly tumbled backward. "You apologize!"

When the professor didn't speak up right away, Jackie took a step toward his table. I hopped off my stool, and Ryan was halfway out of his chair when Professor Goodwin expressed his regret.

"I'm sorry. Truly, madam, that was rude and disrespectful of me, and I didn't mean it. I'm simply confused as to what's going on here, and I misplaced my frustrations."

"We're at a loss ourselves." I sat back down since Jackie had returned to her seat. "Seriously, Captain Spencer, Barbara was murdered in Beech Mountain. Why are you conducting inquiries in Winter Garden?"

Captain Spencer rubbed his forehead. "I guess since we're being honest, I might as well tell you that my chief took me off the case. I had a few personal days I needed to take anyway, so I came here hoping that you or Scott might remember something helpful—maybe an incident you deemed insignificant that took place in the kitchen that morning—and that I could return to Beech Mountain with a solid lead."

"Well, now, we're gonna help you any way we can." Aunt Bess patted his hand again. "Would you like me to have a word with your chief? I can be terribly persuasive."

"No! Please don't call anyone!"

Sheriff Billings had another coughing fit.

"I understand. It'll look better if the chief thinks you didn't have any help." She pretended to lock her lips and throw away the key. "You can count on us not to say a word."

"Thank you, Bess."

"Now, let's get back to business because we're burning daylight." She nodded at Professor Goodwin. "You were telling us how you knew Barbara Hayter."

"I met her Friday night at dinner," he said. "I'd never seen her before that, and I didn't see her after."

"Why did you drive all the way here to ask about my research?" Scott asked him. "You're the historian. I'm only a cake decorator who stumbled across a local legend and integrated it into my design."

"But your cake had sophisticated details," Professor Goodwin said. "I've studied that tale of buried Civil War gold, but I never encountered any reports of a trail marker tree. Did you make that up?"

"No. That tree is one of the few still in existence in the United States, and it's found along the Great Trading Path." Scott shrugged. "I read an account that included the tree, and I was fascinated. I knew that tree belonged on my cake. It's not like I found a treasure map or anything."

"I wish you had," Bill said. "And I'm sorry you were taken off the case, Captain. For what it's worth, I believe you were doing a fine job." He turned his attention to Aunt Bess. "I won't speak for my wife, but Katherine and I met Barbara when she became our realtor. As you've pointed out, she was an odd bird, but I liked her all right. She was a competent realtor, so far as I could tell."

"I liked Barbara," Katherine said. "I'm still horrified that she was murdered in our kitchen. I feel there had to have been something we should have done to better ensure the safety of our guests."

Noticing tears spilling onto her cheeks, I handed her some napkins.

"How many times do I have to tell you, Kathy, there was nothing we could do?" Bill ran a hand through his thinning hair. "We couldn't have possibly anticipated someone coming in and whacking Barbara with a cast-iron skillet. Don't you agree, Captain?"

"Yes, of course. You shouldn't blame yourself for Barbara's murder," he said. "However, going forward, there are precautions you can take to keep anyone from coming onto your property or into your lodge without your knowledge. We can discuss safety measures later."

"That's rather like shutting the barn door after the cow is out, isn't it?" Katherine sniffled into the napkin.

"It is, but it makes sure no other cows go roaming." Captain Spencer gave her a sympathetic smile. "This murder came as a shock to all of us. You weren't the only ones caught woefully unprepared."

My eyes met Ryan's. I knew that he, like I, was wondering what Captain Spencer had or hadn't done to be thrown off the case. We were so not going to the movies tonight.

# Chapter Twelve

Ryan called me after he returned to the sheriff's office. "I know our plans changed while we were in that meeting. Do we want our brainstorming session to be just the two of us, or are we inviting friends?"

"I adore how well we know each other," I said. "Let me check with Mom. If she hasn't got anything going on this evening, we could ask to meet there. Plus, giving credit where credit is due, Aunt Bess has made some keen observations about this case."

"She has. Even though Sheriff Billings almost choked on his coffee twice while trying not to laugh as she took over for Captain Spencer." There was a chuckle in his voice.

"Almost? He spit coffee all over the table once." I laughed. "But then, I sort of felt like somebody needed to take over for Captain Spencer. This whole situation is strange, Ryan."

"I know. We'll figure it out. Let me know how many people you're expecting, and I'll go to Brea Ridge and pick up some food. The last thing you want to do this evening is cater a dinner party."

"Thank you."

After talking with Ryan, I called Mom. "What are you doing this evening?"

"That's a loaded question if I've ever heard one. What am I doing?"

"Ryan and I would love to have a few friends over."

"Here rather than at your place?" she asked.

"Yes. It's like this—we had a meeting today at the café after the close of business."

"I know. Aunt Bess told me all about it…well, her version anyway."

"She's actually providing some good insights into this case, Mom. That's why we want to include her in this discussion."

"What I don't understand is how a Beech Mountain murder became a Winter Garden problem."

"Neither do we, and that's the issue we're trying to figure out," I said. "If you'd rather, we'll meet here at my house, and—"

"No, meet here. If you gather at your house, I'd still have to bring Aunt Bess down there when she saw all the cars in your driveway anyhow, so it makes more sense for you to be here."

"Thanks. Ryan offered to go to Brea Ridge and pick up something for dinner. How about I ask him to bring a party pack from that Mexican restaurant you like?"

"Oh, I do love that place. And so does Clark. May I invite him?

"Absolutely." I paused. "I'd rather you didn't mention our little get-together to Jackie, though."

"Why's that? Did you two have a falling out?"

"Not exactly, but I don't think she's thrilled about Aunt Bess's involvement in this murder investigation."

"Well, I'm not tickled pink that any of you are involved, but I'm not angry about it." She clicked her tongue. "Come to think of it, she did become disproportionately fired up this morning when she called me and asked why Aunt Bess wasn't answering her phone."

"Yeah, she seemed livid when she stormed into the café to get Aunt Bess. To leave school like that was crazy." I huffed. "Surely, she knows I'd never let anything happen to Aunt Bess. And we were at my café not huddled in a foxhole taking mortar rounds. Aunt Bess was perfectly happy."

"All right. I won't say anything to Jackie, and I'll tell Aunt Bess not to mention it if she talks with Jackie either. But, honey, Jackie is going to be angry and hurt if she gets wind of our having a dinner party and not inviting her."

"We're not having a dinner party so much as we're having a meeting of the minds…with food," I said. "But I'd rather handle her irritation later if I must instead of confronting it now. At the moment, I need to figure out why so many Yona guests have followed us home to Winter Garden."

"Okay. Does six o'clock work for everybody?"

"That's fantastic. I appreciate your doing this."

"I want you to be safe," she said.

"Me, too."

After calling Ryan back and filling him in on the plan, I called Scott.

"What's up, Amy-girl?"

"What are you doing this evening?"

"There's this awesome cake competition coming on Food Network later. Wanna come watch it with me? Or wait. Are you asking me because you need me for something?"

I explained the idea Ryan and I had come up with to meet at the big house and try to discover why half the ski lodge guests, plus the proprietors, Captain Spencer, and

Sylvie had come to Winter Garden. Also, I sweetened the pot with the offer of Mexican cuisine.

"That's phenomenal. I'm to the point where I wish we'd never even catered that stupid, non-event."

"I feel you. Do you think Leslie would like to join us?"

"Nah, she's spending the evening with her family."

"Okay." I wondered why he wasn't joining her. Had he not been invited? Was it still too early in their relationship for them to attend each other's family functions? Deciding I was making mountains out of molehills when we hadn't yet even scaled the summit in front of us, I merely told Scott we'd look forward to seeing him at six.

So, we had Ryan, Scott, Aunt Bess, Mom, and Clark. Who else could be a valuable addition to our discussion? Scott's sister, Ivy, certainly would be; but since she'd already put in a full day's work and had a toddler at home, I didn't want to impose on her.

Jackie would be helpful if she wasn't being weirdly antagonistic today. After all, it was she who'd raised the possibility that Barbara ate nothing but a head of lettuce because she was afraid of being poisoned.

I knew I could call Jackie and ask what was wrong with her; but dialing up anyone and asking, 'Hey, what's wrong with you?' guaranteed a response that would be neither warm nor fuzzy. And that question would provoke someone with Jackie's temper even more. No, it was best for me to wait until she'd decided to come talk with me. I didn't want to risk either of us saying something in anger that we might not be able to recover from.

Moving on down my mental checklist, the next logical choice was Sarah. Sarah was the administrative assistant to Billy Hancock, the only attorney with an office in Winter Garden. Even though Billy's specialty was family law rather than criminal law, Sarah was one sharp cookie who had a knack for getting to the crux of a matter while weeding out irrelevant details. Plus, the two of us had been friends since we were knee-high to a grasshopper, and I hadn't seen her in over a week.

"Hey, there," I said, when she answered my call. "Are you up for some Mexican food and a bit of deductive reasoning?"

Laughing, she responded, "You know I am."

"How about John?" Sarah's boyfriend attended law school at the University of Virginia at Wise.

"I'm afraid we'll have to make do without his monster brain. He's at school cramming for mid-terms."

"Well, we'll still have *your* monster brain, so we won't be shortchanged in that department."

"What's going on?" she asked.

I gave her the *Reader's Digest* condensed books' version of the events of the past few days.

"Fascinating. I'm looking forward to this evening," she said. "I'll see you soon."

As I ended the call, a wave of misgiving washed over me. I'd feel better about the upcoming dinner and rehashing of Barbara Hayter's murder if I was optimistic about a positive outcome. But how could we solve the murder of—or even gain any insights into—a woman none of us knew?

I had Captain Spencer's card, and I could have invited him to meet with us. However, although neither Ryan nor I had expressed the feeling outright, I knew neither of us completely trusted him.

Why had his chief removed him from the case? Did Captain Spencer have a personal connection to Barbara? Or had he done something the chief had felt was detrimental to the investigation?

I'd just finished getting ready when I heard a knock at my door. I was thinking it was Ryan, and I opened the door with a broad smile on my upturned face.

It wasn't Ryan. It was Scott. My smile faded as I took in the dark expression on his face and the note in his hand.

"Here." He handed me the note. "Read this."

*Tell me where the Civil War gold is. I know you know more than you're letting on. Cooperate with me, and I'll give you a finder's fee. Don't, and you're in for a world of trouble.*

The unsigned note was written in block print using blue ink on a piece of plain white paper that could have come from any printer.

"Where did you get this?" I asked.

"I found it underneath the windshield wiper on my car when I went outside to come here."

"Do you have any idea who put it there?"

He shook his head. "I looked for footprints, but there were so many around that I couldn't tell one from another."

Giving him a reassuring hug, I said, "Well, at least, we have something new to discuss over dinner."

# Chapter Thirteen

Ryan arrived at my house not long after I read Scott's note. I started to show Ryan the note, but Scott convinced me to wait. Mom, Clark, Aunt Bess, and Sarah were already at the big house waiting for us, and we needed to get the food up there.

We arranged the food buffet-style in the kitchen so everyone could grab a plate, fill it as they wished, and then sit at the dining room table. Mom filled glasses with sweet tea, soda, and water as the guests gave her requests.

Soon, we were all seated in the dining room with plates heaping with tacos, fajitas, mini-quesadillas, and tortilla chips with salsa, guacamole, queso, or a combination of the three.

"This is nice." Aunt Bess beamed at us. "We should do this more often, even when there's not a murder to be solved."

"Where should we begin?" Mom asked. "Clark, Sarah, and I only know the bare minimum about the case. Ryan, have you been able to look into the Beech Mountain Police Department's files?"

Ryan wiped his mouth on his napkin before answering. "I haven't personally accessed any records, but Sheriff Billings did call the Beech Mountain PD earlier today and expressed his concern about individuals who are suspects or at least persons of interest in a homicide that occurred at the Yona Ski Lodge descending upon his town."

"I love all that official, highfalutin language," Aunt Bess said.

"I thought you might," Ryan said, with a grin.

"Did Sheriff Billings tell the Beech Mountain police that Captain Spencer is here too?" I asked.

"I'm not sure." Ryan took a drink of his soda. "I got the impression he wants to get that story straight from the horse's mouth. I wouldn't be surprised if he hasn't already spoken with Captain Spencer privately."

"So, what did the sheriff learn from the Beech Mountain Police Department?" Clark asked.

"Basically, they told him they didn't presume that any of the people Sheriff Billings mentioned posed a direct threat to the residents of Winter Garden but that it wouldn't hurt to keep an eye on them."

"Typical bureaucratic answer." Sarah dipped a chip in queso.

I looked at Scott.

He raised his brows. "You suppose I should go ahead and tell them now?"

As I was nodding, Aunt Bess jumped in to say, "Sweetie, if you've got news, don't keep it to yourself."

Scott took the note that he'd found tucked beneath his windshield, unfolded it, and placed it onto the table. "I got this today. It was on my car, and unfortunately, I don't have a clue as to who put it there."

Ryan, who was sitting to Scott's left, picked up the note. "May I read this aloud?"

Shrugging, Scott said, "Sure."

After reading the note, Ryan said, "I don't like this. I need to tell the sheriff you're being threatened, Scott."

"Do we have to? I mean, isn't it possible it was a joke?" Scott sighed. "If we tell Sheriff Billings, then Ivy will know; and she has enough to concern herself with as it is."

"But we don't know that your note didn't come from the same person who killed Barbara Hayter," Mom said. "Your life could be in danger."

"I doubt it." Scott picked up his glass. "I feel like the people who followed me back to Winter Garden believe I have some kind of inside information on a buried treasure that might not even exist." He raised the glass to his lips and downed the rest of his water. "I can't imagine Barbara's death had anything to do with buried treasure. Does anyone else?" He got up and went to the kitchen to refill his glass.

Sarah waited for Scott to return before making an observation. "The note could be a red herring. Barbara's killer could have put the note on Scott's car to make him and Captain Spencer believe that the ski lodge runaways are only here because they're under the impression that Scott knows where this supposed Civil War gold is buried."

"That's an excellent point, Sarah," Clark said, "but we can't rule out the possibility that at least one of those ski lodge runaways *does* have a suspicion that Scott has some lead on that gold that nobody else knows about."

"And, my dear boy, we can't ignore the fact that the same person who left that note for you might've been convinced that Barbara had the inside scoop herself," Aunt Bess said. "After all, as a realtor, wouldn't she have had access to all sorts of information about the property she was selling? For whatever reason, somebody is fixated on the notion that there's a fortune in gold buried somewhere on the Yona property."

Playing devil's advocate, I asked, "But what if Sarah is right that the note was meant to throw us off the killer's scent? One, why would Barbara's murderer even be here if he or she didn't think one of us saw something incriminating? If Scott is correct, and the treasure hunter and the murderer are two different people, then once we convince them that Scott knows nothing about where any treasure is buried, won't they go away and let us get back to our lives?"

"You'd think so," Ryan said. "But it's unusual that these people all converged on Winter Garden at once—immediately after the ski lodge where they were staying became a murder scene. If they'd all gone to Banner Elk or Sugar Mountain, that would make sense. But Winter Garden?" He shook his head. "Come on. Any way you draw it up, I'm afraid the three of you won't be safe until Barbara Hayter's killer is caught or until our visitors go back to wherever it is they came from."

"Well, you've sure given me something to haunt my dreams tonight," I said. "Jackie must feel the same way you do. That could explain why she's been acting so angry."

"Humph, she's not *acting*," Aunt Bess said. "That girl was fuming when she drove me home today. I half expected to see smoke coming out of her ears."

"Then we'll stay at home tomorrow and put her mind at ease," Mom said.

Aunt Bess shot her a look that plainly said we'll see about that.

"What about this Captain Spencer?" Sarah asked. "What sort of vibe do you get from him?"

Placing her hand on her chest, Aunt Bess said, "I believe he's a good man who has found himself in a bad situation. He's not as experienced with murder investigations as some of us are, but I would love to know why his commanding officer took him off Barbara's case."

"Maybe Barbara sold him a house or something," Scott said. "Wouldn't that make it a conflict of interest for him to investigate her murder?"

"Possibly," Ryan said. "And if he felt she did him dirty in a real estate transaction, he could be a suspect."

We ate in silence for a few minutes after Ryan's statement. He'd given us all something else to mull over. I supposed it was as possible that a police officer could have murdered Barbara as easily as anyone else at the ski lodge. Plus, he'd know how to hide it better. Maybe his fish-out-of-water persona when it came to investigating the murder was all an act. After all, he'd lied to us about his real reason for coming to Winter Garden. He'd said he was here to further investigate the murder…to ask us more questions. Yet he'd been taken off the case. I knew movies and television would have us believe that cops go rogue to solve crimes all the time, especially when doing things by the book isn't accomplishing anything; but how often did that happen in real life?

# Chapter Fourteen

The alarm went off Wednesday morning and yanked me from the depths of the hard-won slumber I so desperately needed. Without opening my eyes, I fumbled on the nightstand until I was able to make the infernal noise stop. Then I rolled back over, pulled the covers up to my chin, and promptly fell back to sleep.

Had it not been for sweet Rory insistently licking my face, I don't know how much longer I'd have stayed in bed. Panic set in as soon as I looked at the clock. I'd overslept half an hour.

I quickly kissed Rory and thanked him for his diligence before jumping out of bed and running to the kitchen to feed him and Princess Eloise. After taking the fastest shower I could manage, I threw on jeans and a sweater, pulled my hair into a ponytail, and hurried to the car. I said a quick prayer of thanksgiving that there wasn't any frost on the windshield as I got in and started the engine.

The absurd thought crossed my mind that I hoped no one would go into my house for some reason today and discover that I hadn't made my bed before leaving this morning. I imagined robbers breaking in through the front door, Princess Eloise hissing at them before running to hide while Rory played in the fenced backyard blissfully unaware of the robbery. The robbers would be disappointed in their potential loot—cookbooks, pet toys, and some vintage board games—and then they'd find the unmade bed.

"What a slob!" Robber One would exclaim.

Maybe Robber Two would be more sympathetic. "Nah, the rest of the house is okay. She probably had to take off in a rush."

Had I been there to explain myself to those imaginary thieves, I could have told them that I'd tossed and turned all night, tormented by dreams of Barbara Hayter, heads of lettuce, and giant cast-iron skillets and that I'd only fallen into a restful sleep moments before the alarm sounded. At least, that's how it had felt.

I arrived at the café and was surprised Scott wasn't there yet. I hoped he hadn't had more trouble with his tires. I hadn't asked him at the time, but I wondered now if the mechanics had checked Scott's other tires when they replaced the one that had gone flat. Surely, they would have, both for Scott's safety and for their potential profit.

My call to Scott went to his voicemail, but I didn't leave a message. I decided he was probably talking with someone else, and I was confident I'd hear from him soon.

I went on into the café, locking the door behind me. Ryan's ominous warning about Aunt Bess, Scott, and me needing to use extra precautions until Barbara's killer was caught or until our guests from Beech Mountain had returned to wherever they called home continued to echo in my brain.

After hanging up my coat and setting all three coffee pots to brewing, I tried Scott's cell phone again. No answer.

Putting on my headset, I went into the kitchen to start breakfast prep. As I got out a mixing bowl, I called Ryan.

"Good morning, beautiful." He sounded as if he'd gotten a great night's sleep, and I was glad for him.

After greeting Ryan, I said, "I'm worried about Scott. He had a flat tire Monday morning, and he isn't here yet and isn't answering his phone. I'm afraid he might be broken down on the side of the road somewhere."

"I'll check it out and give you a call as soon as I can. Let me know if he turns up, all right?"

"Okay, thanks."

We said our goodbyes, and I resumed making biscuits, confident that Scott was fine and that Ryan would find him if he'd had any sort of car trouble this morning.

Hearing a key turn the lock a few minutes later, I glanced over my shoulder, almost certain that Scott had arrived. It was Luis.

"Hi. Want me to lock the door back?"

I looked up at the clock. "No, thanks. It's close enough to time to open that Walter and Dilly should be rolling in any minute now."

"Where's Scott? Is he off today?"

"He wasn't scheduled to be off work, and I'm a little concerned about him," I said. "I'd feel better if he'd answer his phone, but my calls go directly to voice mail."

"Do you want me to go see if he's at home?" Luis asked. "It wouldn't take me long."

"I appreciate that, but Ryan is checking on him already."

"I hope everything is all right." He shrugged out of his coat and hung it up.

I tried calling Scott again. My call went to voice mail. I hung up and tried Ryan. He didn't answer either. I was more worried than ever.

I was only about halfway through breakfast prep when Dilly and Walter arrived. Fortunately, Wednesdays were typically less busy than other days of the week, but I still hated being unprepared.

Dilly had known me long enough she could see right away that something was wrong. "Amy, honey, what is it?"

I gave her and Walter a summary of the morning's events. "I still haven't heard from Scott, and now I can't reach Ryan either."

"I've offered to help Amy out in the kitchen, but I'm not much of a cook," Luis said. "Plus, she doesn't want me to go out looking for Scott and Ryan because she's afraid she'll lose me too."

"You're doing fine." Dilly patted him on the shoulder. "You concentrate on taking orders, bussing tables, and pouring coffee."

"What can I do?" Walter asked, addressing his wife instead of me.

"You help Luis and run the register." Dilly came into the kitchen, washed her hands, tied on an apron, and put on some disposable gloves.

I watched her with my mouth hanging open.

"Finish your breakfast prep while I get started on filling the display case. I can at least bake up some cookies, brownies, and cupcakes."

"But—"

"Get back to work," she said gently.

"Thank you."

"You're welcome." She smiled. "We're all going to keep ourselves busy until we know for a fact that Scott and Ryan are all right, and then Walter and I are going to have breakfast on the house and talk about how much fun it was playing café for a while."

I gave her a quick hug, thanked her again, and dove back into my work.

Although I was still feeling anxious about Scott and Ryan, hungry customers soon filled the café and kept me too busy to try calling either of the men again. Dilly kept reassuring me that everything would be fine.

It was just after eight o'clock, and I was plating a brie and bacon omelet when Jackie stalked into the kitchen.

"Why didn't you call me?" she asked.

"About what?" I garnished the plate with a strawberry rose, put the plate in the server window, and rang the bell.

"About being short-handed."

"I'm not," I said. "Dilly, Walter, and Luis are doing a wonderful job. Besides, I thought you were in class."

"Did you think I was in class last night?" she asked.

Luis dinged the bell letting me know a new order was up. I reached past Jackie to get the slip of paper off the carousel.

"I don't know what you were doing last night." The order was for sausage, eggs, biscuits, and gravy. I stepped back in front of the grill.

"I know what I *wasn't* doing."

"Jackie, I don't know what I've done to you, but you've been angry for two days. Unfortunately, I can't have this conversation right now. Either put on an apron and get to work or get out of the kitchen please."

"Oh! I'm not good enough to come to your dinner party, and now I'm not even fit to be in your kitchen?" Her fists were clenched at her sides.

"You know I didn't say that. I asked you to either help or get out of the way." I put two sausage patties on the grill. "I'm dealing with all I can handle at the moment."

"Well, you don't have to deal with me anymore." She raised her chin. "I quit."

"Jackie!"

She marched out of the kitchen.

I couldn't leave the grill to chase her through the dining room, so I simply let her go.

Dilly took a pan of fresh biscuits from the oven and placed them on the cooling rack. "She'll simmer down and come back to apologize before the day is out. You'll see."

I wasn't even sure what I'd done to her, other than fail to invite her to dinner and ask Mom and Aunt Bess not to mention it to her. Jackie really hadn't been herself since yesterday morning. I hoped she and Roger weren't having problems, but even if they were, she shouldn't take her feelings out on me and the rest of the family.

With a sigh of defeat, I scrambled two eggs for my customer. If I didn't keep busy, I'd fall apart.

When I set the breakfast platter in the serving window, I saw Ryan sitting at the counter.

My heart in my throat, I hurried out of the kitchen. "What's going on?"

"I found Scott's car about two miles from here."

"Then he *did* break down?" I frowned. "Why didn't he answer his phone then? Why didn't he call Luis or me to come pick him up? Was he out there in the cold?"

Ryan stood and put his hands on my shoulders. "The phone was in the car, but Scott wasn't there."

I peered into his eyes. "What are you not telling me? Is Scott all right?"

"We're looking for him."

Drawing in a ragged breath, I asked, "Did he have a wreck? Was he thrown from the car?"

"No, sweetheart. The car is fine. Scott is missing."

# Chapter Fifteen

Shaking off my stupor, I said, "We have to find him." I could either cry and wring my hands, or I could do something productive. "I'll close the café. Homer will still need his sausage biscuit, of course. I'll go ahead and make it and—"

"Amy."

"—take it to his house so he'll have it at ten-thirty. Then—"

"Amy!" Ryan's voice was sharper and more commanding the second time he said my name.

I blinked at him in confusion. "What?"

"You have to stay here."

"No, I need to find Scott."

"We have enough people scouring Winter Garden for Scott," Ryan said. "We need you here asking every person who comes through the door if they've seen him."

"Maybe he got sick while he was driving, and some Good Samaritan stopped and took him to the hospital," I said. "Have you checked the nearby hospitals?"

"We're working on it." His eyes shifted to something or someone behind me, and I whipped my head around to see that Walter, Dilly, and Luis were all standing there.

"Scott's all right. I know he is." The tears I was rapidly trying to blink away belied my words as my brain kept racing. I faced Ryan again. "What about Leslie? Maybe she knows what's going on."

"Ivy has gone to talk with her."

"Ivy." I raised my hand to my mouth. "Poor Ivy…out there looking for her missing brother. Tell her I'm sorry. I'm so sorry, Ryan."

He pulled me into his strong embrace. "Sweetheart, you have nothing to apologize for. Just please keep the café open so we can use it as a central location and can ask anybody passing through if they've seen anything. Will you do that?"

I nodded. "We need a photo."

"We have some flyers, and Captain Spencer has volunteered to stay here at the café and check with everyone coming in as to whether they've seen Scott today." He tipped my chin up to look into my eyes. "We're all praying this is a big overreaction."

"How did Captain Spencer know Scott is missing?" I asked.

"Sheriff Billings called him. We need all the help we can get."

Taking a deep breath, I said, "I'll do whatever I can to make sure Scott comes home safely, including keeping the café open for as long as you need it. We have plenty of food—I'll make sure all the officers and volunteers are fed."

"Thank you." He kissed my forehead. "I have to go."

As Ryan left, I gazed around the dining room. Most of the faces were familiar, but some weren't. Even the clatter of silverware had ceased as Ryan and I had been talking, so I knew the diners had heard at least some of our conversation.

I pulled out a chair and stepped up onto it. Luis slid over to my side, ready to catch me if I should fall.

"For those of you who couldn't hear, Scott is missing. If you come to the Down South Café on a regular basis, then you know Scott well. Deputy Hall says Scott's car was found abandoned with his phone inside, but they can't locate Scott." I clasped my hands together to try to help steady my nerves. "For anyone here who doesn't know Scott, please see Captain Spencer and take a look at the flyer with Scott's photo and description. We need you to help us bring Scott home. Thank you."

Luis helped me down from the chair. "He'll be okay, Amy. He has to be."

The young man was terrified. I squeezed his hand before letting it go. "I know he will." I even managed a brave smile. It was as fake as the one he gave me in return.

Approaching Captain Spencer, I tried not to look at the flyer. I was scared that seeing Scott's photo might make me break down.

"Sir, we have coffee, tea, soft drinks, water, and whatever you'd like to eat."

"I'm not hungry, but I'd love a glass of water."

"Of course. Anything else you need, please let me know." I headed over to get the water, but Walter met me with it halfway. "Thanks. I don't know what I'd have done without you and Dilly today."

"We don't know what we'd do without you every day." He winked and went to check on a table of college students.

I'd barely made it back to the kitchen before Jackie strode in.

"I'm sorry." She put on her apron. "We can talk later, but at the moment, I need to help you and Dilly fill these orders."

"I appreciate it."

She merely bobbed her head and grabbed an order from the carousel.

Homer came in at about a quarter after ten looking as somber as I'd ever seen him.

"You've heard?" I placed a cup of coffee in front of him.

He nodded. "I've been helping to look. I'll go back as soon as I've eaten."

"Does your hero of the day have any words that might strengthen us?" I asked.

"I imagine he'd probably say something along the lines of, 'Chill out, dudes. It's all good. Everything will be fine.'"

Tears pricked my eyes and made my nose burn. His hero was Scott. I patted Homer's hand and then hurried into the kitchen to prepare his sausage biscuit.

Dilly started to hug me.

"Please don't," I whispered. "I'll break into a million pieces."

"I understand." She put a sausage patty onto the grill. "Why don't you step outside for a second and get some fresh air?"

"I'll do that. Thanks."

I went out the back door and looked down at the little bird tracks in the otherwise undisturbed snow. Making a mental note to put out some seeds, I marveled at how my mind could go to such a mundane place in the midst of worrying about Scott. I supposed it was a coping mechanism, a way to concentrate on anything except the circumstance I couldn't fix.

Had Scott gone directly home after leaving the big house last night? Or had he possibly gone to see Leslie?

What difference did it make either way? His car had been found only a couple of miles from here. If the car hadn't stopped working, why had Scott pulled off the road? Since Ryan hadn't said anything about the car not working or having something obviously wrong with it like a flat tire or smoke pouring out from under the hood, I was guessing it wasn't car trouble that had made Scott drive to the shoulder of the road and stop.

So, what *had* been the impetus for Scott's actions? Had he encountered another motorist in distress? Seen an injured animal on the side of the road and stopped to help? Whatever it was that had compelled Scott to stop his car and get out must have either seemed safe for him to do or else he felt it was something he had to do for someone or something else. He wouldn't have taken an unnecessary risk for no good reason, especially not after our dinner where Ryan warned him, Aunt Bess, and me to be on our guard until Barbara Hayter's killer was caught.

I shivered. There were no answers to be found out here in the cold. I might as well get back inside and begin prepping for the lunch crowd. Hopefully, someone had seen something helpful on their way to work today.

When I plodded back into the kitchen, Jackie said, "Leslie and her aunt are here to see you."

I rushed into the dining room. "Leslie, Daphne, do you have any news about Scott?"

Leslie shook her head. It was apparent from her swollen eyes that she'd been crying.

"I know you're busy," Daphne said, "but can you spare us ten minutes?"

"Absolutely. In fact, I was going to close the café altogether today, but Ryan pointed out that by staying open we could ask people if they'd seen something that can help us find Scott." I didn't want her and Leslie to think I didn't care about Scott's welfare and that I was keeping the café going as if it were any other day.

"I agree with Ryan," Daphne said.

"May I get you something to eat or drink?" I asked.

Both declined.

"Did anything weird happen at dinner last night?" Leslie asked. "I know you were meeting to discuss that realtor lady's murder and to try to understand why so many people from the ski lodge have turned up in Winter Garden. Did you come to any conclusions?"

"Nothing solid," I said. "Did Scott mention the note he received?"

"About the treasure?" she asked. "Yeah, he told me."

"We aren't sure if the note was legitimate or not."

Daphne frowned. "You suppose it was a joke?"

"Actually, the thought crossed our minds that Barbara Hayter's killer could be using the treasure as a smoke screen and that leaving the note for Scott was intended to throw everyone off the real reason for the murder, especially since Captain Spencer is in town."

"We noticed that." Daphne gave Captain Spencer an appraising stare that lasted long enough for him to catch her. She raised her hand in a slight wave.

"That's stupid," Leslie said. "Why is an officer from another jurisdiction hanging out here in Winter Garden?"

I lowered my voice. "His commanding officer took him off the case."

"Any idea why?" Daphne asked.

"Not a clue, but it would have to be either some sort of conflict of interest or inappropriate behavior regarding the case, wouldn't it?"

"I'd imagine." Daphne shot another look in Captain Spencer's direction. "My sister, Violet, is a realtor. I'll see if she's ever heard of Barbara Hayter. Could we meet after you close up today, provided Scott hasn't been found by then?"

"Yes. I'd love to do something more proactive than cook eggs and pancakes."

"Don't underestimate what you're doing here," Daphne said. "A lot of people drove up and down that road where Scott's car was found this morning, presumably around the same time he went missing. Let's hope and pray some of those people come in here for lunch and can tell us what they know."

# Chapter Sixteen

At three o'clock that afternoon, I flipped the *Open* sign to *Closed* and studied the people sitting in the dining room. Captain Spencer was sitting alone and was examining his fingernails. Ryan and Sheriff Billings were talking with Ivy. Dilly and Walter were sitting with Mom, Clark, and Aunt Bess. Jackie, Roger, Sarah, and Homer sat together and appeared to be deep in conversation. Leslie, her aunt, Daphne, and a woman I was guessing to be Leslie's mom, Violet, sat quietly at a table off to the side.

"What do we do now?" I asked.

Thankfully, Sheriff Billings had a response. "The Winter Garden Sheriff's Office's second and third shifts will continue searching for Scott throughout the evening. Captain Spencer and I will be driving to the Yona Ski

Lodge to learn if anyone in the vicinity has seen Scott, since his disappearance aligns with the presence of some dubious visitors to Winter Garden. I hope the remainder of you will go home, rest, and keep your spirits up. Ivy, Leslie, Amy, I'll call each of you if and as soon as I hear something."

"Just please don't let on to Mom," Ivy said. "If she knew Scott was missing, it would kill her."

"Captain Spencer, are you ready?" Sheriff Billings asked.

The other man stood. "Yes, sir."

"Ryan, call me if anyone here needs me." With that last instruction, Sheriff Billings and Captain Spencer left.

I went over to the table where Ryan sat with Ivy.

Sitting beside Ivy, I placed my hand on hers. "Is there anything I can do?"

"Just pray," she said. "At this point, I don't know what else to do."

"I imagine everyone in Winter Garden is praying for Scott." I squeezed her hand. "We'll find him."

"I've never felt so helpless in all my life. Scott is my baby brother. I'm supposed to protect him." She pushed back her chair. "I need to get home and make sure Mom doesn't find out about Scott's disappearance—at least, not until we know what we're up against. I'll see you tomorrow."

"Has anyone from the Sheriff's Department been able to reach any of the Yona guests?" I asked Ryan after Ivy left.

"One of our deputies spoke with Katherine," Ryan said. "She and Bill have returned to the lodge. Someone was able to speak with Professor Goodwin, but the others weren't answering their phones."

"Not even Sylvie?" I raised my eyebrows. "She runs a taxi service. How could she not answer her phone?"

He shrugged. "Maybe she was off today. Lots of people take a day off mid-week when they work weekends."

From the corner of my eye, I saw Aunt Bess opening her mouth to speak. Never knowing what Aunt Bess might say, I cut her off before she could say something alarming. "Is anyone hungry?"

"My friends texted me that they were taking care of that." Aunt Bess smiled broadly as a fire truck pulled up outside the café. "And here they are now."

She all but floated to the door and held it open as members of the Winter Garden Fire Department brought in boxes of food. Three muscular, handsome men placed the food on the counter.

"We even brought paper plates and napkins," one said, with a wink at Aunt Bess. "Didn't want you to have to worry about cleanup."

"These are ham, turkey, and roast beef subs, a variety of chips, and gallons of sweet tea, unsweet tea, and lemonade—all from the sandwich shop in Brea Ridge," another said.

"You're angels; that's what you are." Aunt Bess pulled on his arm until he bent down low enough for her to kiss his cheek.

"We truly appreciate this," I said. "How much—"

"Don't even finish that thought," he said.

Another firefighter stood in the center of the dining room. Raising her voice to be heard above the ongoing conversations, she asked, "Could I please have everyone's attention for a moment? We want you to know that not only are we remaining vigilant in the search for Scott, but we've reached out to fire stations within a hundred-mile radius of here, and they're also looking for him."

As most of the other people lined up for food, I went over to speak with Leslie, Daphne, and the woman I believed to be Violet. If so, the sisters were a contrast of dark and light. Daphne with her dark hair worn sleek and straight; Violet with her blonde curls. Under different circumstances, I could easily imagine Violet being the life of the party while Daphne would be content to sit in a quiet corner and observe everyone else.

"Hi," I said, as I approached the table.

"Hello, Amy. I'm Violet. I've heard wonderful things about you."

"Thank you. I—"

"Take a seat," Daphne said. "We need to leave soon, and I want us to have the opportunity to discuss Barbara Hayter's murder and how it might or might not be connected to Scott's disappearance."

I understood Daphne's urgency, but I wasn't going to be outdone. "I've heard wonderful things about you too, Violet." I pulled out a chair and sat. "Did you know Barbara?"

"I didn't," Violet said. "I grasped from Daphne and Leslie that the people who visited Winter Garden these past couple of days following Barbara Hayter's murder were all interested in some Civil War gold believed to be buried on or around the ski lodge property and which they felt Scott possibly had some knowledge about."

"All because he alluded to a local legend on his cake," Leslie said. "How dumb are these people?"

"I agree that a cake is a far cry from a treasure map," I said. "And I'm not so sure all of them were here trying to get Scott to lead them to the gold. For instance, one man—Doug something-or-other—said he and his family were in Winter Garden because they were visiting relatives in Brea Ridge."

I didn't mention Sylvie, who I also thought had other reasons for making the trip. Scott might not have mentioned Sylvie to Leslie, and I didn't want to give

Leslie any sort of erroneous indication that he and Sylvie could have taken off somewhere together.

"Who was here asking about the gold?" Daphne asked.

"The only person who seriously sought Scott out to question him about his research into the legend was Professor Charles Goodwin," I answered.

"He was the only person who seriously asked." Daphne frowned slightly. "Were there others who joked about it?"

"Bill and Katherine, the ski lodge proprietors, kidded about it—mainly Bill. I felt like he was pretty much trying to lighten the mood because Katherine was still shaken. She's the one who found Barbara."

"If there was any truth to the legend of the buried gold, then the realtor could very well have read about it while researching the deed to the property," Violet said. "With a piece of land located in the North Carolina mountains where there is more than one gem mine tourist attraction, one of the first avenues I'd have explored would have been the property's mineral and surface rights."

"I hadn't even thought of that," I said.

"Many buyers don't, but if they take possession of a property on which underground resources are discovered, they could be in for a rude awakening if they discover after the fact that someone else holds the land's mineral rights." She shook her head. "I always do my best to verify that my clients aren't in for any hasty surprises somewhere down the road. If Barbara Hayter was worth her salt as a realtor, so did she. Mineral rights don't apply to buried treasure, but if she was doing a deep dive on the property's history, she should have come across the story."

"But if she'd learned about the possibility of there being buried treasure on the land, wouldn't she have told her clients?" Leslie asked.

"She should have." Violet shrugged. "Perhaps she did—or maybe she wrote the legend off as an old wives' tale."

I remembered Barbara talking about the farm she'd buy should she find gold. She hadn't made any mention that evening of having prior knowledge of the legend other than saying it was a rumor. Had she simply wanted to go along with the rest of us, joking about how we'd spend the money?

"Or she could have been planning to search for the gold herself," Daphne said. "Back to the people who were at the lodge and then wound up in Winter Garden—I'm guessing the police contacted all of them?"

"All of them they were able to reach." I motioned Ryan over.

He excused himself from Homer and Roger, with whom he'd been speaking, and came to the table.

"Ryan, you know Leslie. This is her mom, Violet, and her aunt, Daphne."

"Daphne's Delectable Cakes." He took a chair from another table and sat down. "Your reputation precedes you. It's a pleasure to meet you both, but I'm sorry it's under these circumstances."

"Likewise," Daphne said. "Were the police able to visit with all the people from Beech Mountain who ended up coming to Winter Garden after Barbara Hayter's murder? I'm wondering if the Beech Mountain Police Department followed up with them in person, maybe tracked down anyone you were unable to reach by phone."

Ryan stiffened. "We're working closely with the Beech Mountain Police Department as well as with other agencies in the region. Everyone here is dedicated to bringing Scott home safely."

"I know you are," she said. "I'm sorry. I didn't mean to sound crabby. I'm frustrated that there isn't something more I can do."

"We all are." He stood.

"We need to go. Jason and Luke will be home soon, and they'll want to know the latest information." Violet got to her feet and reached out a hand for Ryan to shake. "Thank you for all your hard work. We appreciate you."

"You're welcome."

As soon as he'd shook Violet's hand, Leslie gave him a hug.

"Drive safely," he said.

As Leslie, Violet, and Daphne left the café, Ryan put his arms around me, and I buried my face against his chest. How intensely I wished I could wake up and find that this entire day had been a terrible nightmare.

# Chapter Seventeen

Ryan followed me to my house. After feeding Rory and Princess Eloise, we sat on the sofa. We didn't watch television. We didn't talk. We simply held each other.

When my phone buzzed, I started so violently that I nearly came up out of my seat.

"Hello? Hello?"

I realized then that my phone hadn't rung, it had buzzed, indicating I'd received a text. Feeling like an idiot, I opened my messages and read the text.

"It's from Violet," I told Ryan. "She has a friend who is a realtor in North Carolina. Her friend looked up the information for the Yona ski lodge property."

"That quickly?"

"Yeah. The friend had been the selling agent on the property a few years ago, but the sellers changed their minds. Anyway, Violet says there's a hidden bunker located on the lower southwest quadrant of the property." I raised my head. "We've got to go. I'd bet you dollars to doughnuts that's where we'll find Scott."

"That's a long shot, but since Sheriff Billings is already in Beech Mountain, I'll call him and have him check out the bunker."

"If he feels Scott might be there, can we go?" I asked. "If Scott is in that bunker, I want him to see a friendly face when he comes out."

"You don't think Sheriff Billings has a friendly face?"

"Not as friendly as mine." My gaze didn't waver.

"Let me see what the sheriff says." He'd already taken out his phone. Now he pulled up his contacts and called Sheriff Billings.

"Ryan, what've you got?"

With his phone on speaker, I could hear Sheriff Billings too.

"I'm here with Amy, sir. Leslie's mother is a realtor, and she just now texted Amy and said there's a hidden bunker in the lower southwest quadrant of the ski lodge property."

"That's a fairly vague description," the sheriff said.

Ryan's brows knitted together. "I'm aware of that, but if we can pull together a search and rescue team from the area, we should be able to find the bunker in no time even in the dark."

"I see. Did the witness say whether or not this person fitting Scott's description was alone?"

A chill coursed through my body. Something was wrong. Something was very wrong.

"I understand," Ryan said. "Are you in Beech Mountain?"

"Sure."

"Still with Captain Spencer?"

"Yep."

"You no longer trust him?"

"That's sharp, Deputy Hall. Have someone check it out."

"I'll get you some help out there as quickly as I can."

"I appreciate that," Sheriff Billings said. "Please give me a call if you get any more leads or if this tip pans out."

"Are you in immediate danger, sir?"

"Nah, the captain and I will stick to our original plan to visit the ski lodge and the surrounding area unless you call us back to say that was indeed Scott our witness saw." He gave a humorless chuckle. "Good thing we're in the captain's SUV. My squad car sure wouldn't have made it up this mountain."

"All right. See you soon." Ryan ended the call and looked at me. "He's in trouble."

"I could tell, but I don't believe the captain realizes yet that he no longer has Sheriff Billings' trust."

"Maybe not, but it's only a matter of time."

"What's the plan?" I asked.

"We have a new utility vehicle at the Sheriff's Department. I'm going to go get it and head to Beech Mountain."

"I'm going with you."

"No, you're not," he said. "I appreciate your concern and your willingness to help, but this is a potentially dangerous situation. Having you with me would jeopardize your safety and distract me from doing my job."

"You're right." I stood on my tiptoes and gave him a quick kiss. "Please be careful."

"For real? You're giving in that easily?"

"Yes. You definitely don't need to be distracted. Is there anyone I can call for you or anything else I can do to help?"

"No, I'll coordinate with other agencies on the drive to Beech Mountain," he said. "I love you, Amy."

"I love you." I stood in the doorway, waved goodbye, and watched him leave.

Then I immediately called Roger.

"Hey, Flowerpot."

Roger had given me the irritating nickname when we were children, and he was the only person who'd ever been allowed to use it.

"Is your truck four-wheel drive?" I asked.

"Yeeeesss." He drew out the word as if he wanted to give himself a second to comprehend why I was calling. He lowered his voice. "You know I'm at the big house right now, don't you?"

"I don't care where you are. Just come and get me, and don't tell anyone else where you're going."

"Easier said than done."

"Roger, please, this is urgent, and we need to hurry."

"All right."

Once I had his confirmation that he'd be here, I ended the call and raced to the bedroom to put on some thick socks and a pair of boots. Rory watched me, his scruffy head tilting first one way and then the other.

"Don't give me that look. I know I shouldn't be trailing along behind Ryan like this, but he'll get there long before Roger and I do. He and Sheriff Billings can sort out Captain Spencer, and then Roger and I can join in the search for Scott."

Rory gave a little bark of agreement…or excitement…or saying, "You are completely out of your mind."

I kissed his head. "I know. I know! But I have to do something!"

I put on my coat, hat, and gloves and was standing on the front porch with my purse when Roger arrived.

Launching myself down the steps and into the driveway, I flung open the passenger side door, saw Jackie, and shut it back again. I went around to the driver's side.

Roger put down his window. "Yes?"

"Has Jackie talked you out of taking me to Beech Mountain?"

"No." Jerking his head in the direction of the backseat, he said, "Get in."

I opened the door and climbed in, grateful that Roger's truck was so roomy. As I buckled my seatbelt, I briefly explained about Violet's text and Ryan's call to Sheriff Billings.

"Ryan is on his way. He went to the station first to get the utility vehicle, and he was planning on coordinating with other law enforcement agencies while he drove," I said. "If Scott is in that bunker, I want to be there to make sure he's all right."

Jackie swiveled in her seat so she could see me. "I want to be there too. We all care about Scott."

"I realize that. If you're ticked off because I asked Roger not to tell anyone where he was going, I said that because I didn't want Aunt Bess to find out. You know as well as I do that she'd be sitting right back here beside me if she knew what we're doing."

"True, and she'll pout for days at us for going off and leaving her."

"There's no guarantee we'll even find Scott there," Roger said. "This feels like a wasted effort to me."

"I have a hunch that's where he's at," I said. "But even if he isn't, Sheriff Billings is in trouble."

"And Ryan is on his way to help him." Roger looked into the rearview mirror and held my gaze for a moment. "We're only going to be in the way."

"But if Sheriff Billings suspects Captain Spencer of killing Barbara and taking Scott, then even if Scott isn't at the lodge, Captain Spencer knows where he is," I said.

"It's conjecture, Flowerpot, and it's pretty flimsy."

"You're backing out?"

He sighed. "No. I'll take you to Beech Mountain…if for no other reason than to get you two to have the heart-to-heart you need to have."

"A heart-to-heart about what?" I asked Jackie. "The reason you're angry with me?"

"I haven't been angry with you. I've been angry at myself."

"Over what?" I looked back into the mirror at Roger's reflection for some sort of clue as to what Jackie was talking about, but his eyes were firmly on the road.

Jackie sighed. "School. I'm flunking out."

"What? Why? I thought you were doing so well."

"I guess I liked the core courses and electives more than I did the courses pertaining to my major," she said. "I don't think I'm cut out to be a bookkeeper or an accountant. Crunching numbers all day long would drive me bonkers."

"Does Aunt Bess know?"

"No one but Roger knows."

"What do you want to do now?" I asked.

She faced the front again. "I have no idea."

This time when I searched for Roger's eyes in the rearview mirror, I found them. She did know what she wanted to do. So did he.

# Chapter Eighteen

The Yona Ski Lodge nestled among the snowy mountains and framed by towering fir trees exuded the picturesque charm of a Bob Ross painting. But a slight turn of the head revealed an unsettling contrast, transforming the picturesque setting into something reminiscent of a scene from a true crime show.

Law enforcement vehicles dotted the landscape, their lights strobing red and blue on the snow-covered ground. As a handcuffed Captain Spencer was being placed in the back of a Beech Mountain Police Department SUV, Sheriff Billings and Ryan approached the white pickup truck they recognized as belonging to Roger.

“Y’all might as well get out,” Sheriff Billings said.

Roger opened his door and got out of the truck. "Evening, Sheriff Billings."

"Where is she?" Ryan asked. "I know Amy put you up to this."

I got out of the truck. "Hi. Are you mad?"

"Mad doesn't begin to describe how I'm feeling right now," he said. "But that's a conversation for another time."

"Right," Sheriff Billings said. "We still have work to do."

"So, no sign of Scott?" I asked.

"Not yet, but we've got a crew searching for that bunker." The sheriff ran a hand down his face. "We're hoping, based on what Spencer has told us, that we'll find Scott there."

Jackie had joined us now. "What was Spencer's deal? Did he kill Barbara?"

"He didn't, but he's been manipulating the investigation from the start." Sheriff Billings explained how he'd been suspicious of Captain Spencer from the moment the officer showed up in Winter Garden. "I contacted his chief and asked why he'd been taken off the Barbara Hayter murder investigation. Spencer's chief said that Spencer didn't even take anyone's fingerprints as a way to eliminate or confirm them as the murderer. Had he done that, the case would have been resolved because the killer left fingerprints all over that skillet."

"That's right," I said. "No one took our fingerprints."

"On the drive up here, I asked Spencer about the investigation, and he got awfully squirrelly about the whole thing. I knew he was involved somehow, but I didn't know how. He finally confessed that the killer had begun blackmailing him as soon as he'd arrived at the ski lodge."

"How?" Roger asked. "I mean, if the killer is blackmailing an officer, that's even better than a confession, isn't it?"

"Well, you'd think so, but Barbara's murderer called Spencer on his cellphone and told him that if he didn't botch the investigation, everyone on the police force would find out that Spencer had broken his wife's leg in a domestic assault that he'd managed to keep out of court."

"How would the killer know about the captain's assault on his wife?" Jackie asked.

"Because he was a physical therapist," I said.

Sheriff Billings nodded. "Bingo."

"Where's Doug now?" I asked.

"We don't know," Ryan said. "Hopefully, we'll find him with Scott."

In the distance, we saw a flare go up.

"They've found the bunker," Sheriff Billings said, striding in the direction of the flare.

"Ryan?" I began.

"Come on," he said, gruffly. "But stay behind us and out of harm's way."

I wasn't sure what I was expecting, but the bunker looked like a cellar to me. It was dark and dank and musty, and then—

"Scott!"

At least ten law enforcement officers turned to glare at me while the others kept their eyes on their suspect. I wasn't intimidated. I squeezed around to the side of the group where I could get a better look at Scott.

He appeared to be okay. His eyes were trained on the officers, and their eyes were trained on Sylvie.

"Sylvie?"

Roger grabbed my arm and tugged me backward. "Hush."

"I was trying to help," Sylvie said, her arms high in the air. "Please don't shoot me. I promise I didn't have anything to do with Doug's killing Barbara or kidnapping Scott. I'd never hurt Scott—or anybody!"

"It's true—the part about trying to help me," Scott said. "She came here to find me after she realized what Doug had done."

"How'd you know what Doug had done?" Sheriff Billings asked.

"Initially, he, Barbara, and I were going to search for the gold and split the proceeds. We'd talked about it last year when Barbara first found out there was supposedly gold buried on this land." Sylvie's eyes darted from one officer to another. "She'd told Doug about the legend in my cab. Her mother was his patient, and they were going to lunch to discuss her treatment. Barbara thought the whole thing about the gold was a joke until Doug convinced her that there was a strong possibility that the story was true."

"And they took you on to buy your silence?" the sheriff asked.

"Not really. I believe they were afraid I'd find it first," she said.

"There wasn't a lot to find." Scott reached into his pocket and withdrew a worn brown pouch. "Five one-dollar gold coins circa 1861." He tossed the pouch to Sheriff Billings.

"Where'd you get this?" Sheriff Billings asked.

Scott shrugged. "I had to do something while I was locked in this place all day. I found the treasure."

"Sylvie, do you have any idea where Doug is now?" Ryan asked.

She shook her head. "He was supposed to be coming here. I'm guessing seeing all the law enforcement vehicles scared him off."

We began trudging back through the snow to the lodge. Scott needed to get warm and to eat something before returning to Winter Garden. He was also eager to call Ivy and Leslie and let them know he was all right.

At the lodge, the law enforcement officers who'd escorted us from the bunker dispersed and said they'd be on the lookout for Doug.

Scott, Ryan, Sylvie, Jackie, Roger, Sheriff Billings, and I stepped inside the lodge. There in the lobby, hidden from the view of the windows, Doug was holding Katherine with a knife against her throat.

"If you don't want this woman's blood on your hands, Sheriff, you'll give me that pouch of gold you're holding and let me leave here."

"Son, this gold isn't what you think it is," Sheriff Billings said. "I'd say it's worth about thirty-five hundred dollars, tops."

"You're lying! Hand it over!"

Ryan looked at a spot behind Doug and nodded.

Doug whirled around with the knife raised to attack the person he thought was taking direction from Ryan.

Ryan rushed Doug, as Bill pulled Katherine to safety. After wrestling the knife from Doug's hand, Ryan handcuffed the man.

I felt my knees go weak and might've sunk onto the floor had Jackie not put a comforting arm around me.

"Thanks," I whispered.

"Anytime."

# Chapter Nineteen

The next morning, we didn't open the Down South Café until nine o'clock. I'd called Dilly the night before to give her the good news about Scott and had told her we'd be sleeping in just a bit. She was delighted and said she and Walter would see us around nine-thirty.

Scott, naturally, had the day off, but Jackie and I were planning a celebration for him later that day. Since he'd found the treasure, Katherine and Bill had given him the gold coins. He kept one, gave two to Katherine and Bill, gave one to me, and proudly presented the final one to Aunt Bess.

Luis was filling salt and pepper shakers when Ryan came into the café.

"Morning, Luis. Give Amy and me a minute, would you?"

I took a steadying breath. Ryan and I hadn't spoken last night, except for when I'd told him how very proud I was of him. He'd given me a curt *thanks* and kept walking.

So, here goes that conversation we couldn't have at the ski lodge last night. Would he express his anger and disappointment? Or would he flat-out tell me he never wanted to see me again?

"Would you like coffee?" I asked.

"No, thank you." He took my hand and walked me over to a table in the back corner. "Sit down."

I opened my mouth to speak, but I had no idea what to say.

"I promise this won't take long," he said.

Nodding, I pulled out a chair and took a seat. "I'm sorry."

"No, you're not. You're hardheaded, obstinate, and loyal to a fault. I honestly believe you'd fight a tiger over someone you care about."

"Ryan, I'm—"

"Let me finish," he interrupted.

I nodded and lowered my gaze to my hands.

"Look at me."

Sighing, I raised my eyes.

"You drive me up the wall, Amy. You frustrate the living daylights out of me, you know that?" He lowered himself onto one knee. "But I love you with all my heart, and I can't live without you." He took a small velvet box from his pocket and opened it to reveal an emerald and diamond engagement ring. "What do you say, will you drive me crazy for the rest of my life?"

"I will!"

"Thank goodness!" Luis said from his vantage point in the server window.

Leslie arrived with our sheepish hero after everyone else was in place for the party. It wasn't much of a surprise, but he was touched, nonetheless. In addition to "the regulars," half the town had turned out to welcome Scott home and to tell him how much he meant to them.

I sidled next to Jackie. "Come with me. We're going to steal Scott for a second."

"Um…I think that's already been done, and it was a nightmare for everybody," she said.

Slapping my hand to my forehead, I said, "Bad choice of words."

She grinned. "You think?"

"Come on." I tugged her along with me to Scott's side. "I need to *borrow* you for a moment. Would you please join Jackie and me in the kitchen?"

"Sure. Lead the way."

I hadn't been wearing my engagement ring all day because I'd been afraid of losing it. Now I took it from my pocket and slid it onto my finger.

Jackie gasped and hugged me. "Congratulations!"

"I'm happy for you, Amy-girl." Scott hugged me as soon as Jackie let me go. "Do I get to be the best man?"

"That's between you and Ryan. I have to say, though, I know that you and Jackie are certainly the best."

"Right back atcha," Scott said.

"I don't want to lose either one of you." I gave a nervous chuckle. "I guess it's a day of proposals all around. I'd like for both of you to be my partners in the Down South Café."

They looked at me, then at each other, and back at me.

"I do!" they said in unison.

In the midst of the group hug, I said a silent prayer of thanksgiving for the wonderful people with whom I was going to be sharing my future.

# What's Cooking at the Down South Café?

Tarte a L'orange – From Quaint French Living: https://quaintfrenchliving.com/the-best-classic-french-orange-tart-recipe-tarte-a-lorange/

Cherokee Fry Bread – From Just A Pinch: https://www.justapinch.com/recipes/bread/bread-flatbread/cherokee-fry-bread-recipe.html

Scottish Oatmeal Rolls – From Taste of Home: https://www.tasteofhome.com/recipes/scottish-oatmeal-rolls/

German Pork Schnitzel – From The Daring Gourmet: https://www.daringgourmet.com/traditional-german-pork-schnitzel/

Hopping John – From Immaculate Bites: https://www.africanbites.com/hopping-john/

Irish Roasted Salmon – From The Café Sucre Farine: https://thecafesucrefarine.com/irish-roasted-salmon/

English Scones – From Unpeeled Journal: https://unpeeledjournal.com/buckingham-palace-english-royal-scones-recipe/

Buckwheat Pancakes – From Inspired Taste: https://www.inspiredtaste.net/38616/buckwheat-pancakes/

Bacon and Brie Omelette – From Simply Delicious: https://simply-delicious-food.com/brie-and-bacon-omelette/

Go back and read any of the Down South Café mysteries that you might've missed! See the list of books in order at https://www.gayleleeson.com/down-south-cafe-mystery-series

After the list of books and the author section, please read the first chapter of DESIGNS ON MURDER, book one in the Ghostly Fashionista Mystery Series.

# Also by Gayle Leeson

## Down South Café Mystery Series

The Calamity Café
Silence of the Jams
Honey-Baked Homicide
Apples and Alibis
Fruit Baskets and Holiday Caskets
Truffles and Tragedy
Pickled to Death (novella)

## Ghostly Fashionista Mystery Series

Designs on Murder
Perils and Lace
Christmas Cloches and Corpses
Buttons and Blows
Secrets and Sequins

## Literatia Series (Written as G. Leeson)

Saving Piglet (prequel)

An Eyre of Mystery

A Tale of Two Enemies

The Legend of Creepy Hollow (short story)

## Movie Memorabilia Series

Terminated: He Won't Be Back (prequel)

We'll Always Have Murder

## Kinsey Falls Chick-Lit Series

Hightail It to Kinsey Falls

Putting Down Roots in Kinsey Falls

Sleighing It in Kinsey Falls

## Victoria Square Series (With Lorraine Bartlett)

Yule Be Dead

Murder Ink

Murderous Misconception

Dead Man's Hand

## Embroidery Mystery Series (Written as Amanda Lee)

The Quick and The Thread

Stitch Me Deadly
Thread Reckoning
The Long Stitch Goodnight
Thread on Arrival
Cross-Stitch Before Dying
Thread End
Wicked Stitch
The Stitching Hour
Better Off Thread

## Cake Decorating Mystery Series (Written as Gayle Trent)

Murder Takes the Cake
Dead Pan
Killer Sweet Tooth
Battered to Death
Killer Wedding Cake

## Myrtle Crumb Mystery Series (Written as Gayle Trent)

The Party Line (prequel)
Between A Clutch and A Hard Place
When Good Bras Go Bad
Claus of Death
Soup…Er…Myrtle!
Perp and Circumstance

# ABOUT THE AUTHOR

Gayle Leeson is known for her cozy mysteries. She also writes as Gayle Trent and Amanda Lee. To eliminate confusion going forward, Gayle is writing under the name Gayle Leeson only. She and her family live in Southwest Virginia with Cooper, the Great Pyrenees in the photograph with Gayle, and a small pride of lions (cats, really, but humor them).

If you enjoyed this book, Gayle would appreciate your leaving a review. If you don't know what to say, there is a handy book review guide at her site (https://www.gayleleeson.com/book-review-form). Gayle invites you to sign up for her newsletter and receive excerpts of some of her books: https://forms.aweber.com/form/14/1780369214.htm

**Social Media Links:**
Twitter:

https://twitter.com/GayleTrent

Facebook:

https://www.facebook.com/GayleLeeson/

BookBub:

https://www.bookbub.com/profile/gayle-leeson

Goodreads:

https://www.goodreads.com/author/show/426208.Gayle_Trent

# Have You Met Max, the Ghostly Fashionista?

## Excerpt from *Designs on Murder*

# Chapter One

A flash of brilliant light burst from the lower righthand window of Shops on Main, drawing my attention to the FOR LEASE sign. I'd always loved the building and couldn't resist going inside to see the space available.

I opened the front door to the charming old mansion, which had started life as a private home in the late 1800s and had had many incarnations since then. I turned right to open another door to go into the vacant office.

"Why so glum, chum?" asked a tall, attractive woman with a dark brown bob and an impish grin. She stood near the window wearing a rather fancy mauve gown for the middle of the day. She was also wearing a headband with a peacock feather, making her look like a flapper from the

1920s. I wondered if she might be going to some sort of party after work. Either that, or this woman was quite the eccentric.

"I just came from a job interview," I said.

"Ah. Don't think it went well, huh?"

"Actually, I think it did. But I'm not sure I want to be doing that kind of work for...well...forever."

"Nothing's forever, darling. But you've come to the right place. My name's Max, by the way. Maxine, actually, but I hate that stuffy old name. Maxine Englebright. Isn't that a mouthful? You can see why I prefer Max."

I chuckled. "It's nice to meet you, Max. I'm Amanda Tucker."

"So, Amanda Tucker," Max said, moving over to the middle of the room, "what's your dream job?"

"I know it'll sound stupid. I shouldn't have even wandered in here--"

"Stop that please. Negativity gets us nowhere."

Max sounded like a school teacher then, and I tried to assess her age. Although she somehow seemed older, she didn't look much more than my twenty-four years. I'd put her at about thirty...if that. Since she was looking at me expectantly, I tried to give a better answer to her question.

"I want to fill a niche...to make some sort of difference," I said. "I want to do something fun, exciting...something I'd look forward to doing every day."

"And you're considering starting your own business?"

"That was my initial thought upon seeing that this space is for lease. I love this building…always have."

"What sort of business are you thinking you'd like to put here?" Max asked.

"I enjoy fashion design, but my parents discouraged me because—they said—it was as hard to break into as professional sports. I told them there are a lot of people in professional sports, but they said, 'Only the best, Mandy.'"

Max gave an indignant little bark. "Oh, that's hooey! But I can identify. My folks never thought I'd amount to much. Come to think of it, I guess I didn't." She threw back her head and laughed.

"Oh, well, I wish I could see some of your designs."

"You can. I have a couple of my latest right here on my phone." I took my cell phone from my purse and pulled up the two designs I'd photographed the day before. The first dress had a small pink and green floral print on a navy background, shawl collar, three-quarter length sleeves, and A-line skirt. "I love vintage styles."

"This is gorgeous! I'd love to have a dress like this."

"Really?"

"Yeah. What else ya got?" Max asked.

My other design was an emerald 1930s-style bias cut evening gown with a plunging halter neckline and a back panel with pearl buttons that began at the middle of the back on each side and went to the waist.

Max caught her breath. "That's the berries, kid!"

"Thanks." I could feel the color rising in my cheeks. Max might throw out some odd phrases, but I could tell she liked the dress. "Mom and Dad are probably right, though. Despite the fact that I use modern fabrics—some with quirky, unusual patterns—how could I be sure I'd have the clientele to actually support a business?"

"Are you kidding me? People would love to have their very own fashion designer here in little ol' Abingdon."

"You really think so? Is it the kind of place you'd visit?" I asked.

"Visit?" Max laughed. "Darling, I'd practically live in it."

"All right. I'll think about it."

"Think quickly please. There was someone in here earlier today looking at the space. He wants to sell cigars and tobacco products. Pew. The smell would drive me screwy. I'd much rather have you here."

Hmm...the lady had her sales pitch down. I had to give her that. "How much is the rent?"

"Oh, I have no idea. You'll find Mrs. Meacham at the top of the stairs, last door on your left. It's marked OFFICE."

"Okay. I'll go up and talk with her."

"Good luck, buttercup!"

I was smiling and shaking my head as I mounted the stairs. Max was a character. I thought she'd be a fun person to have around.

Since the office wasn't a retail space like the other rooms in the building, I knocked and waited for a response before entering.

Mrs. Meacham was a plump, prim woman with short, curly white hair and sharp blue eyes. She looked at me over the top of her reading glasses. "How may I help you?"

"I'm interested in the space for rent downstairs," I said.

"You are? Oh, my! I thought you were here selling cookies or something. You look so young." Mrs. Meacham laughed at her own joke, so I faked a chortle to be polite. "What type of shop are you considering?"

"A fashion boutique."

"Fashion?"

"Yes, I design and create retro-style fashions."

"Hmm. I never picked up sewing myself. I've never been big on crafts." She stood and opened a file cabinet to the left of her desk, and I could see she was wearing a navy suit. "Canning and baking were more my strengths. I suppose you could say I prefer the kitchen to the hearth." She laughed again, and I chuckled along with her.

She turned and handed me an application. "Just read this over and call me back if you have any questions. If you're interested in the space, please let me know as soon as possible. There's a gentleman interested in opening a cigar store there." She tapped a pen on her desk blotter. "But even if he gets here before you do, we'll have another opening by the first of the month. The web designer across the hall is leaving. Would you like to take a look at his place before you decide?"

"No, I'd really prefer the shop on the ground floor," I said.

"All right. Well, I hope to hear from you soon."

I left then. I stopped back by the space for lease to say goodbye to Max, but she was gone.

I went home—my parents' home actually, but they moved to Florida for Dad's job more than two years ago, so it was basically mine...until they wanted it back. I made popcorn for lunch, read over Mrs. Meacham's contract, and started crunching the numbers.

I'd graduated in May with a bachelor's degree in business administration with a concentration in marketing and entrepreneurship but just couldn't find a position that sparked any sort of passion in me. This morning I'd had yet another interview where I'd been overqualified for the position but felt I had a good chance of getting an offer...a low offer...for work I couldn't see myself investing decades doing.

Jasmine, my cat, wandered into the room. She'd eaten some kibble from her bowl in the kitchen and was now interested in what I was having. She hopped onto the coffee table, peeped into the popcorn bowl, and turned away dismissively to clean her paws. She was a beautiful gray and white striped tabby. Her feet were white, and she looked as if she were wearing socks of varying lengths—crew socks on the back, anklets on the front.

"What do you think, Jazzy?" I asked. "Should I open a fashion boutique?"

She looked over her shoulder at me for a second before resuming her paw-licking. I didn't know if that was a yes or a no.

Even though I'd gone to school for four years to learn all about how to open, manage, and provide inventory for a small business, I researched for the remainder of the afternoon. I checked out the stats on independent designers in the United States and fashion boutiques in Virginia. There weren't many in the Southwest Virginia region, so I knew I'd have something unique to offer my clientele.

Finally, Jazzy let me know that she'd been napping long enough and that we needed to do something. Mainly,

I needed to feed her again, and she wanted to eat. But I had other ideas.

"Jazzy, let's get your carrier. You and I are going to see Grandpa Dave."

Grandpa Dave was my favorite person on the planet, and Jazzy thought pretty highly of him herself. He lived only about ten minutes away from us. He was farther out in the country and had a bigger home than we did. Jazzy and I were happy in our little three-bedroom, one bath ranch. We secretly hoped Dad wouldn't lose the job that had taken him and Mom to Florida and that they'd love it too much to leave when he retired because we'd gotten used to having the extra space.

I put the carrier on the backseat of my green sedan. It was a cute car that I'd worked the summer between high school and college to get enough money to make the down payment on, but it felt kinda ironic to be driving a cat around in a car that reminded people of a hamster cage.

Sometimes, I wished my Mom and Dad's house was a bit farther from town. It was so peaceful out here in the country. Fences, pastureland, and cows bordered each side of the road. There were a few houses here and there, but most of the land was still farmland. The farmhouses were back off the road and closer to the barns.

When we pulled into Grandpa Dave's long driveway, Jazzy meowed.

"Yes," I told her. "We're here."

Grandpa Dave lived about fifty yards off the road, and his property was fenced, but he didn't keep any animals. He'd turned the barn that had been on the land when he and Grandma Jodie bought it into a workshop where he liked to "piddle."

I pulled around to the side of the house and was happy to see that, rather than piddling in the workshop, Grandpa was sitting on one of the white rocking chairs on the porch. I parked and got out, opened the door to both the car and the carrier for Jazzy, and she ran straight to hop onto his lap.

"Well, there's my girls!" Grandpa Dave laughed.

It seemed to me that Grandpa was almost always laughing. He'd lost a little of that laughter after Grandma Jodie had died. But that was five years ago, and, except for some moments of misty remembrance, he was back to his old self.

I gave him a hug and a kiss on the cheek before settling onto the swing.

"I was sorta expecting you today," he said. "How'd the interview go?"

"It went fine, I guess, but I'm not sure Integrated Manufacturing Technologies is for me. The boss was nice, and the offices are beautiful, but...I don't know."

"What ain't she telling me, Jazzy?"

The cat looked up at him adoringly before butting her head against his chin.

"I'm...um...I'm thinking about starting my own business." I didn't venture a glance at Grandpa Dave right away. I wasn't sure I wanted to know what he was thinking. I figured he was thinking I'd come to ask for money--which I had, money and advice—but I was emphatic it was going to be a loan.

Grandpa had already insisted on paying my college tuition and wouldn't hear of my paying him back. This time, I was giving him no choice in the matter. Either he'd lend me the money, and sign the loan agreement I'd drafted, or I wouldn't take it.

I finally raised my eyes to look at his face, and he was looking pensive.

"Tell me what brought this on," he said.

I told him about wandering into Shops on Main after my interview and meeting Maxine Englebright. "She loved the designs I showed her and seemed to think I could do well if I opened a boutique there. I went upstairs and got an application from the building manager, and then I went home and did some research. I'd never seriously considered opening my own business before--at least, not at this stage of my career--but I'd like to try."

Another glance at Grandpa Dave told me he was still listening but might take more convincing.

"I realize I'm young, and I'm aware that more than half of all small businesses fail in the first four years. But I've got a degree that says I'm qualified to manage a business. Why not manage my own?"

He remained quiet.

"I know that opening a fashion boutique might seem frivolous, but there aren't a lot of designers in this region. I believe I could fill a need…or at least a niche."

Grandpa sat Jazzy onto the porch and stood. Without a word, he went into the house.

Jazzy looked up at me. *Meow*? She went over to the door to see where Grandpa Dave went. *Meow*? She stood on her hind legs and peered through the door.

"Watch out, Jasmine," he said, waiting for her to hop down and back away before he opened the door. He was carrying his checkbook. "How much do you need?"

"Well, I have some savings, and—"

"That's not what I asked."

"Okay. Now, this will be a loan, Grandpa Dave, not a gift."

"If you don't tell me how much, I'm taking this checkbook back into the house, and we won't discuss it any further."

"Ten thousand dollars," I blurted.

As he was writing the check, he asked, "Have you and Jazzy had your dinner yet?"

We were such frequent guests that he kept her favorite cat food on hand.

"We haven't. Do you have the ingredients to make a pizza?"

He scoffed. "Like I'm ever without pizza-makings." He handed me the check. "By the way, how old is this Max you met today? She sounds like quite a gal."

"She doesn't look all that much older than me. But she seems more worldly…or something. I think you'd like her," I said. "But wait, aren't you still seeing Betsy?"

He shrugged. "Betsy is all right to take to Bingo...but this Max sounds like she could be someone special."

First thing the next morning, I went to the bank to set up a business account for Designs on You. That's what I decided to name my shop. Then I went to Shops on Main and gave Mrs. Meacham my application. After she made sure everything was in order, she took my check for the first month's rent and then took me around to meet the rest of the shop owners.

She introduced me to the upstairs tenants first. There was Janice, who owned Janice's Jewelry. She was of average height but she wore stilettos, had tawny hair with blonde highlights, wore a shirt that was way too tight, and was a big fan of dermal fillers, given her expressionless face.

"Janice, I'd like you to meet Amanda," said Mrs. Meacham. "She's going to be opening a fashion boutique downstairs."

"Fashion? You and I should talk, Amanda. You dress them, and I'll accessorize them." She giggled before turning to pick up a pendant with a large, light green stone. "With your coloring, you'd look lovely in one of these Amazonite necklace and earring sets."

"I'll have to check them out later," I said. "It was nice meeting you."

Janice grabbed a stack of her business cards and pressed them into my hand. "Here. For your clients. I'll be glad to return the favor."

"Great. Thanks."

Next, Mrs. Meacham took me to meet Mark, a web site designer. Everything about Mark screamed thin. The young man didn't appear to have an ounce of fat on his body. He had thinning black hair. He wore a thin crocheted tie. He held out a thin hand for me to shake. His handshake was surprisingly firm.

"Hello. It's a pleasure to meet you, Amanda." He handed me a card from the holder on his desk. "Should you need any web design help or marketing expertise, please call on me. I can work on a flat fee or monthly fee basis, depending on your needs."

"Thank you, but—"

"Are you aware that fifty percent of fledgling businesses fail within the first year?" he asked.

I started to correct his stats, but I didn't want to alienate someone I was going to be working near. I thanked him again and told him I appreciated his offer. It dawned on me as Mrs. Meacham and I were moving on to the next tenant that she'd said the web designer was leaving at the end of the month...which was only a week away. I wondered where he was taking his business.

The other upstairs shop was a bookstore called Antiquated Editions. The owner was a burly, bearded man who'd have looked more at home in a motorcycle shop than selling rare books, but, hey, you can't judge a book by its cover, right?

I made a mental note to tell Grandpa Dave my little joke. As you've probably guessed, I didn't have a lot of friends. Not that I wasn't a friendly person. I had a lot of acquaintances. It was just hard for me to get close to people. I wasn't the type to tell my deepest, darkest secrets to someone I hadn't known...well, all my life.

The brawny book man's name was Ford. I'd have been truly delighted had it been Harley, but had you been expecting me to say his name was Fitzgerald or Melville, please see the aforementioned joke about books and covers. He was friendly and invited me to come around and look at his collection anytime. I promised I'd do so after I got settled in.

Then it was downstairs to meet the rest of the shop owners. The first shop on the left when you came in the door--the shop directly across the hall from mine--was Delightful Home. The proprietress was Connie, who preferred a hug over a handshake.

"Aren't you lovely?" Connie asked.

I did not say I doubt it, which was the first thought that popped into my brain, but I did thank her for the compliment. Connie was herself the embodiment of lovely. She had long, honey blonde hair that she wore in a single braid. Large silver hoops adorned her ears, and she had skinny silver bracelets stacked up each arm. She wore an embroidered red tunic that fell to her thighs, black leggings, and Birkenstocks. But the thing that made her truly lovely wasn't so much her looks but the way she appeared to boldly embrace life. I mean, the instant we met, she embraced me. Her shop smelled of cinnamon and something else…sage, maybe.

"Melba, that blue is definitely your color," Connie said. "By the way, did that sinus blend help you?"

"It did!" Mrs. Meacham turned to me. "Connie has the most wonderful products, not the least of which are her essential oils."

I could see that Connie had an assortment of candles, soaps, lotions, oils, and tea blends. I was curious to see what all she did have, but that would have to wait.

"I'm here to help you in any way I possibly can," said Connie, with a warm smile. "Anything you need, just let me know. We're neighbors now."

Mrs. Meacham took me to meet the last of my "neighbors," Mr. and Mrs. Peterman.

"Call us Ella and Frank," Ella insisted. She was petite with salt-and-pepper hair styled in a pixie cut.

Frank was average height, had a slight paunch, a bulbous nose, and bushy brown hair. He didn't say much.

Ella and Frank had a paper shop. They designed their own greeting cards and stationery, and they sold specialty and novelty items that would appeal to their clientele. For instance, they had socks with book patterns, quotes from famous books, and likenesses of authors.

After I'd met everyone, Mrs. Meacham handed me the keys to my shop and went upstairs. Although my shop wouldn't open until the first of September, she'd graciously given me this last week of August to get everything set up.

I unlocked my door and went inside. I was surprised to see Max standing by the window. I started to ask her how she'd got in, but then I saw that there was another door that led to the kitchen. I imagined my space had once been the family dining room. Anyway, it was apparent that the door between my space and the kitchen hallway had been left unlocked. I'd have to be careful to check that in the future.

But, for now, I didn't mind at all that Max was there. Or that it appeared she was wearing the same outfit she'd been wearing yesterday. Must have been some party!

"So, you leased the shop?" Max asked.

"I did!"

"Congratulations! I wish we could have champagne to celebrate."

I laughed. "Me too, but I'm driving."

Max joined in my laughter. "I'm so glad you're going to be here. I think we'll be great friends."

"I hope so." And I truly did. I immediately envisioned Max as my best friend—the two of us going to lunch together, talking about guys and clothes, shopping together. I reined myself in before I got too carried away.

I surveyed the room. The inside wall to my right had a fireplace. I recalled that all the rooms upstairs had them too. But this one had built-in floor-to-ceiling bookshelves on either side of the fireplace.

"Does this fireplace still work?" I asked Max.

"I imagine it would, but it isn't used anymore. The owners put central heat and air in eons ago."

"Just checking. I mean, I wasn't going to light fire to anything. I merely wanted to be sure it was safe to put flammables on these shelves." I could feel my face getting hot. "I'm sorry. That was a stupid thing to say. I'm just so excited—"

"And I'm excited for you. You have nothing to apologize for. How were you supposed to know whether or not the former tenant ever lit the fireplace?"

"You're really nice."

"And you're too hard on yourself. Must you be brilliant and well-spoken all the time?"

"Well...I'm certainly not, but I'd like to be."

"Tell me what you have in store for this place," she said.

I indicated the window. "I'd like to have a table flanked by chairs on either side here." I bit my lip. "Where's the best place around here to buy some reasonably priced furniture that would go with the overall atmosphere of the building?"

"I have no idea. You should ask Connie."

"Connie?" I was actually checking to make sure I'd heard Max correctly, but it so happened that I'd left the door open and Connie was walking by as I spoke.

"Yes?"

"Max was telling me that you might know of a good furniture place nearby," I said.

"Max?" Connie looked about the room. "Who's Max?"

I whirled around, thinking Max had somehow slipped out of the room. But, nope, there she stood...shaking her head...and putting a finger to her lips.

"Um...she was....she was just here. She was here yesterday too. I assumed she was a Shops on Main regular."

"I don't know her, but I'd love to meet her sometime. As for the furniture, I'd try the antique stores downtown for starters. You might fall in love with just the right piece or two there." She grinned. "I'd better get back to minding the store. Good luck with the furniture shopping!"

Connie pulled the door closed behind her as she left, and I was glad. I turned to Max.

"Gee, that was awkward," she said. "I was sure you knew."

"Knew?"

"That I'm a ghost."

Made in the USA
Columbia, SC
20 January 2024